THE FIERCE SAGA
BOOK TWO

PREVIOUS WORKS

Fantasy:

Guarding Heaven's Gates (15th Year Anniversary Revised Edition releases in 2018)

Science-Fiction / Thiller:

The Fierce Are Fading (*Fierce Saga: Book 1)*

The Fierce Are Fading: The Graphic Novel

UPCOMING WORKS

Science-Fiction / Thiller:

Fury of the Fierce (*Fierce Saga: Book 3*)

THE FIERCE WILL FALL

JOSHUA D. HOWELL

To all those who put up with me then, and continue to do so now.

CONTENTS

Acknowledgments   i

1   Mud and Muck   1

2   Kumbaya   13

3   Sorry, Not Sorry   29

4   Milk Does the Body Good   39

5   Sledgehammer   49

6   There Goes the Freeway   69

7   Hello There   81

8   What's in a Name?   101

9   Care to Dance?   125

10   That Snowden Guy was Right?   147

11   Don't Touch My Food   159

12   Killing at the Playground   177

13   Sit Tight   203

14   There's Blood on the Ivory   209

15   Thirst   227

16   Do You Want to Live?   245

ACKNOWLEDGMENTS

Thank you to my wife and friends for their encouragement and support. Thank you, also, to Katelyn Hertel for editing this book and being a valuable asset to me during the overall writing of this book.

1 MUD & MUCK

If Margaret ever had a purpose in life, she had lost sight of that purpose long ago. In her youth, she left her small town in search for something more; traveled to Vegas to be a part of the show, the big show. The lights engulfed her, the music drowned out her inhibitions, the games enticed her, the liquor quenched her thirst, and the drugs burnt out her worth. When her debts were stacked, and her charm could no longer get her by, she found herself roaming the alleyways and backstreets. She was sleeping on the curbs and bus benches, begging for change outside the market, and rummaging for scraps in the dumpsters behind the pantries and giftshops. She refused to call home for help because she knew the call would fall on deaf ears anyway. She had burnt all her bridges upon leaving, and even at her lowest low, she couldn't envision herself swimming back across that murky water to the place she once called home.

Eventually she left Vegas, and hitched a ride on a hippie bus headed for Nashville. Halfway along the route, however, she was discarded at a truck stop in Oklahoma with a couple bucks, a peanut butter and jelly sandwich, and some half-hearted "good luck" wishes. She used the cash to buy shots from a gas station, and stumbled along the road until she found solace in a ditch beside the highway. Covered in mud and muck, sitting in the dark with nothing to her name but a pair of broken high heels, Margaret laid back and closed her eyes with the hope that she wouldn't ever open them again. The next morning, however, she did.

Margaret woke to a man calling out to her from the side of the road. He was wearing a suit and tie, had a book in his hand, and was slowly trying to make his way down the muddy wall of the ditch. The sun was blaring down from overhead, and it took her a few moments of squinting and rubbing her eyes before she could see clearly. As everything came into focus, she realized that a large commercial bus had stopped on the side of the road and several people were looking out the windows at her. Finally, the man in the suit had made his way down into the ditch and knelt down beside her.

"Miss! Are you alright? Do you need to go to the hospital?" Margaret looked up at him for a moment, admiring the genuine concern in his eyes. He was likely in his mid-forties or fifties, with hints of gray in his hair and gentle wrinkles along his brow. She smiled up at him for a moment before remembering the predicament she was in. Suddenly, a wave of embarrassment came over her as she tried to right herself in the mud.

"I'm fine, I'm fine. I don't need any hospital." Margaret struggled to stand as her feet kept slipping back and forth. The kind man took her arm and helped her to stability.

"Ok. Well, I can't simply leave you here. Is there somewhere you need to go, Miss? Somewhere we can take you?" Margaret looked up at him, then over the bus of people, and then back at him.

"Uh….," Margaret tried to remember what State she was in as she looked down the road in one direction and then down the other; nothing in sight. "Where are you going?"

"Oh, we're going to a special place." The man signaled back to the bus and almost immediately a woman came out with a towel, a large gallon of water, and some clothes. "Why don't you come with us? Sarah here can help you clean up, get you into some clean clothes, and find you a seat on the bus. We've got some snacks in there, and there will be a big dinner tonight. How does that sound?"

Margaret nodded and thanked him. It was truly the first form of kindness she had encountered in a very, very long time. The man helped her out of the ditch and went back to the bus. Sarah and a couple of other girls held a large towel to give Margaret some privacy as they helped her wash off the mud and get into some fresh clothes. As she stood there, nude, washing the grime from her skin while basking in the rays of the sun, she felt an overwhelming sense of relief overtake her.

****

The bus continued to travel across the countryside throughout the majority of the day. Once she had devoured some snacks and drank as much water as she could, Margaret fell asleep to the sounds of the group singing Amazing Grace and Kumbaya. By the time she awoke, it was dark out and the bus was pulling into a field with a large enclosed tent. This tent was similar to the old circus tents; tall and pulled down by ropes and spikes, lit up in the middle. Several other buses, cars, and trucks were there. Once off the bus, Margaret followed the line into the tent where she was given a styrofoam plate, a bottle of water, and offered a buffet of casseroles, fruits and vegetables, and all the other foods she could have imagined. When her plate was stacked high with food, she was ushered further into the tent to a chair facing a small stage where a band was performing. Still a bit speechless at the sight of everything, Margaret dug into her meal and thanked her lucky stars for finding this place.

As the tent began to fill with more and more people, and the food began to run out, the last few stragglers were offered soup and bread and whatever chairs that were left. The band finished up and left the stage as a man with silver hair jumped up on stage and grabbed the microphone. He shook the hands of the band members as they left the stage, gave a motion to the tech booth, and soon enough the lights dimmed and the crowd began to quiet down.

"Welcome strangers! Welcome to a night of purpose and redemption!" The crowd began to cheer, and Margaret just put down her plate and sat quietly. "I see we have a variety of people here, coming from a variety of walks of life. I may not know any of you personally, but I can guarantee that each of you have something in common. You are all struggling with something. It may be big, it may be small, but it's there, and it's been eating you up from the inside for too long now. I can tell you one thing folks, no matter how you came to hear about tonight's event, you were brought here for a reason; for a purpose!

"What purpose could I be talking about? Well, that's for you to figure out personally. Now we are a room full of different people, and we likely don't share the same core beliefs, but I can tell you that no matter if you're ready to admit it, deep deep down you know that there is an emptiness inside of you; something that you know needs to be filled, fixed, changed, before you can go on any further. Well folks, I'm here to tell you that I have the answer that you are looking for. I'm here to tell you just how we are going to fix you up!" Again, the tent erupted in cheers and clapping, but this time, Margaret couldn't help but join in. In a tent filled with a thousand people, she felt like this man was speaking directly to her. "This world has been spinning and spinning around in its own chaos for far too long, and it's starting to come to a halt, ladies and gentlemen. The surface has become heavy with all the laziness and wickedness of the world.

"You know what I'm talking about. The way society has driven us into loneliness and depression, and turned us into slaves to feed the never ending machine. You can't just live on this earth, you have to pay the man for the right to live; electricity bills, home loans, gas for your car, data for your phone, birthday gifts for all your so-called friends, flowers and cards for your loved ones, taxes on your food and your water. It never ends people! We've become trapped under the thumb of the rich and conceited. We've become infected by their products, the must-haves of the world, that we've lost sight of what we really need to survive. I'm here to tell you that there is a higher power that calls upon each of us, you and me, to fix this earth; to rid the world of these evils, and bring it back to the Eden that it was intended to be. This higher power calls on you, and you sir, and you ma'am, and you too!

"A long time ago the Romans referred to this higher power as M.O.R.S., but we know it today as the very Wrath of God. He's angry, ladies and gentlemen. Wouldn't you be? He created a Utopia, and we've muddied it up with all of our shortcomings. There was a time when you didn't need alcohol or drugs to feel happy, when you didn't need to sell yourself for money to get by." Margaret was gripping the edge of her seat. There was a reason she had ended up here, and this man was going to tell her. "It is our duty to be vessels, to be representatives of the Wrath of God, and bring justice once more to this place. But before we can do that, we have to fix what's wrong with ourselves. We have to find our former selves; our cleaner, peaceful, pure selves. But here's the catch folks, and I'm sorry to have to tell you this, but you will never find that side of yourself where you are now, here among the evils of this place.

"So what are you to do? Well, like I said, you were brought here for a purpose, and so was I. My purpose is to invite you to come away with me. There is a place out there, a place where we have found solitude and righteousness. It is the closest thing to the original Eden, and we believe it has been blessed for all of us. There, the waters will cleanse your soul, and the fruits will nourish your younger self. There, you can let go of the burdens that you've acquired over the years, and the vile that you've got stuck under your skin.

"Now there are gentlemen making the rounds throughout this tent. They are going to help you let go of the things that are holding you back. I challenge you to give up your petty belongings, the items that the world has forced you to be captive to. I'm here to remind you that you aren't defined by your phones, or your credit cards, or your debt. None of those things matter where we are going.

"You came here because you were looking for something; that one thing that's missing from your life, and I would bet that you're missing that purpose that I mentioned earlier. When you have a true purpose in life, you will find a peace and redemption that you've never known. You will discover how to live as a whole being again. So, I want you to come with me to this new place to find that redemption that we are all striving for. I know it's scary, but be honest with yourself. When was the last time you made a choice that would save your life, your very soul?

"If you're willing to make that leap, to find your true potential, and come with me to this Eden that we have found! We have a few buses in back that will take you there. We have a few more nights like this, where we are going to be meeting with other people, in other tents, dealing with the same troubles that you are. I'm going to share with them the same message, and I want you to help me convince them that they are not alone! It is a hard choice, but I tell you that if you give yourself freely, there is a grace that will overtake you and show you the way. Thank you all, and I hope to see you again soon."

The crowd roared in applause, and Margaret couldn't help but jump to her feet and add to the noise. She was enthralled by the man's words. Everything he said seemed to apply to her, and although it had been years since she had stepped foot inside a church, outside of the rent-a-wedding joints in Vegas, she felt like she truly believed in what was being preached.

The band took the stage again to end the night. After all the dancing, hollering, and hooting, Margaret followed her new found companions back onto the bus, and the trip continued. They made stops in Arkansas and Mississippi, until they eventually made their way down to Louisiana. It was there that some of the buses got shuffled up a bit and Margaret ended up sitting next to a nice girl with short brown hair named Alissa Lynn.

Alissa wasn't the talkative sort, but as the caravan of buses made their way down through Texas and toward the southern border, the two women stuck close. Eventually, Margaret shared her story with Alissa and in turn, over time, Alissa shared hers. Alissa was apparently on the run from an abusive ex-boyfriend. She was a recovering alcoholic, and she didn't have a dime to her name. Their similar struggles only made the two women closer.

Before the caravans crossed the border into Mexico, each person was given a piece of paper. Everyone was encouraged to write down their name and address, as well as a short letter that would be sent to their loved ones, their friends, or anyone that would wonder where they went. Margaret was hesitant, and could see that Alissa was too. Still, they did as they were told and Margaret felt as if it were simply another layer that she was peeling away to truly free herself.

The journey was longer than most expected, but it didn't deter most people. Through the nights, Alissa and Margaret would switch off, using the other as a pillow. They scavenged for food together, kept each other warm in the cold nights, dry on the boat rides, and sane through the hot afternoons.

Eventually, the group made it down to a large camping ground in the forest outside of Panama. The campus was just a turn off a dirt road and through a gate guarded by men with rifles. After the gate, the road winded through a couple of different orchards, and over a hill before it reached the main facilities. The layout reminded Riley of a military training base. There were barrack structures, large covered shelters with tables and chairs, shower and bathroom units, gardens, and a large three story building in the middle with antennas on top.

It was late in the evening, and so the group was shown to their barracks for the night. Each bed was nicely made with a pillow, sheets, and a thin blanket. At the foot of the bed was a towel and wash cloth, as well as two pairs of cotton pants and matching tops. The clothes were thin and almost transparent, but they appeared to be breathable for the heat. Everyone was told to toss their old clothes in the provided black bags and change into the new approved attire.

Margaret and Alissa paired up at a bunk bed; Margaret took the top. As the lights turned off and the deafening silence took over, Margaret let out a long and heavy sigh. She had finally arrived, and she couldn't wait to wake in the morning and learn everything she could about this new paradise. She would make this place her new home. She would commit to the change that she needed inside. She would become something new.

2 KUMBAYA

CHURCH OF MORS CAMPUS
6 months later

Alissa Lynn woke from her slumber to the short calls of some Sapayoa birds nearby. The sun was just starting to peek through the high open windows of the barracks. She shimmied out of her sheets and climbed out of bed. Margaret, like most of the rest of the barracks, was still sound asleep and looked to be in deep, so Alissa let her be, put on her shoes, and went for her morning run.

As with everything else, this had become a routine for Alissa. On the first morning of their stay, Alissa and the rest of the newcomers were split into groups and assigned to certain factions of the camp. Each faction was instrumental in keeping the camp running. Some worked in the kitchen, some worked in the orchards, some washed laundry in the nearby stream, some worked as part of a construction team that built new structures, while others worked in the garden; Alissa and Margaret were both assigned there.

Every day after that was the same. Alissa would go for her morning jog and then return to the barracks to shower while everyone else slowly got up and made their way to the chow hall for breakfast. After breakfast, everyone would meet in the large clearing, kneel on yoga mats, and partake in a daily communion and blessing before separating off into their assigned groups. The groups would work from 8am to 5pm, breaking for lunch, and at designated times throughout the week for their teaching sessions.

The teaching sessions would differ from week to week. They would consist of a sermon at times, interactive sessions, written or physical tests, and sometimes just silent mediation. Whatever the session consisted of, it held the same message: self-cleansing. Every single person needed to admit that they were there for a reason, that they had something within themselves that needed cleansing, and that they couldn't progress in life until that cleansing had occurred.

Crossing the campus grounds, Alissa waved and smiled toward some passing guards, who broke their resolve briefly to smile back. Once she had cleared the main grounds, Alissa took off in a jog through the orchards. It was only during this time on her run, in the mid-morning, in the quiet, that Alissa truly had time to herself. She took this time to breathe, to relax, and to remind herself of all the details of her mission.

In the six months since she arrived, Alissa had made a point to get the lay of the land. Apart from the main grouping of barracks, learning shelters and chow halls, shower and bathroom buildings, Alissa knew of several other buildings that were off limits to most people. There was a three story building that she had dubbed the control tower, due to the antennas and satellite dish affixed to the roof. The building, which stood in front of the clearing that hosted the morning communion sessions, had one entrance, a steel door secured by pin code. Only the third floor had windows, and they overlooked the clearing.

Other than the control tower, there was a set of buildings about a half mile down a wooded path that Alissa did not have access to. The campers learned quickly that personal cleansing was certainly incentivized, as it came with benefits that the normal

Joshua D. Howell

camper did not get to partake in; private meals, off campus trips, and eventually the ultimate accreditation of being named as one of the "ascended." As the months went by, and more people were bused in, several people would achieve this accreditation.

They would then graduate from the barracks and would move out of the main campus and to the cluster of buildings down the path. These chosen few were praised by the elders among the camp, and upon moving out of the barracks, they were never seen again. In the night, Alissa could hear buses leave the grounds, and so she could only assume that eventually these "ascended" campers were being sent somewhere; to another facility perhaps, or possibly even back to the states.

No matter what she did, Alissa couldn't acquire the coveted special status, and had become surprised at how much it had actually irritated her. She minded her p's and q's, participated in all of the sessions, strived to make the best of her duties, and worked to be a productive member of the camp. She tended the gardens to the best of her abilities with Margaret and the other assigned campers during the weekdays. While she always kept a smile on her face, Alissa's true feelings must have been apparent as Margaret began to call out Alissa's frustrations. Margaret would offer some kind, reassuring words that one day they would both be chosen, but that for now they should cherish their time at the camp.

Margaret clearly adored this place, this new Eden. On the trip down to the campus, and during the first month, she suffered heavy withdrawal from the drugs and alcohol her body had grown to depend on. Alissa was not opposed to their friendship, as it helped her blend in, but she could tell that Margaret fit a certain demographic that the Church of MORS seemed to prey upon; the weak, lost, and easily persuaded. Before long, Margaret was the ideal resident. She was heavily involved in the learning sessions. Alissa watched the gleam in Margaret's eyes as she took in the generally vague sermons about how everyone has a darkness in them, and how all of their problems in life stemmed from their separation from righteousness. Alissa saw right through the thin veil of bullshit, as these "teachers" were using the chemical makeup of religion to draw in the weak-minded to agree with whatever else they were preaching.

Alissa wasn't necessarily an atheist. She had been raised in the church as a child, and would admit to herself that she believed in something, somewhere, but wasn't quick to define it. Over the years she had seen so many horrible things done by extremists who swore up and down that their actions had been ordained by the great one above. She could recognize that these sick few did not reflect the whole of believers, but she also saw how easily verses and scripture could be bent and twisted to meet any person's narrative; just as it was being used by the Church of MORS.

Once she had jogged through the orchards, Alissa normally took a path that led down into the forest south of the campus. The fenced-in grounds spanned in size somewhere between ten and twelve square miles, with thick forest surrounding it on all sides and set apart from any other residential area by several miles. There were guards that walked the outer perimeter, and some guards would simply walk the paths around the grounds. Other than the gate and the path that led to the "chosen" buildings, the grounds weren't overly guarded. One could easily sneak out, but with all the activities during the day, it wouldn't be long until their absence was noticed. Alissa approached a guard that she regularly saw on the south forest path and came to a stop to catch her breath.

"Good morning Simon, how are you today?" The guard took a quick look around to make sure no one else was in ear shot and then smiled back at Alissa.

"You know guards aren't supposed to talk to the residents." Alissa tilted her head and smiled, and Simon rolled his eyes. "I'm doing well Ali. How's the run?"

"Refreshing thank you. You know if you all had a basketball court around here, I could get my exercise in by playing the guards in a bit of a one on one."

"Ha. Yeah, I'll tell the grounds crew to get right on that." A branch cracked in the distance and Simon quickly raised his rifle and scanned the area. Alissa had studied Simon and several of the other guards to determine if they were simply hired help with basic gun knowledge, or if they were more. Simon gave off a boy-scout, military reject type of vibe. He seemed like he could handle his own if the time came. When Simon didn't see anything in the woods, he relaxed his composure and turned back to Alissa.

"Everything alright, Simon?"

"Oh, I'm sure it was nothing but a little critter out there somewhere. Still, you can never be too careful. I wish you'd head back to campus, though." Alissa shook her head and smiled.

"Nope! Now you know I need to get my

running in before communion. I've just got a little bit more to go. I'll see you up there shortly." Simon smiled and rolled his eyes again as he continued on his way.

Alissa stretched a bit more, cracked her neck, and did some jumping jacks until Simon was out of sight. After waiting a few moments more, Alissa jogged a little deeper into the woods away from any other guards or residents. When she was certain that she was alone, she came to halt and peered in the direction of the woods where the branch had cracked. She gave a nod, and slowly, but surely, several men in camouflage rose up from the brush.

"Way to make an entrance. The first time I hear from you guys since I left the states and you almost blew it," she said to the nearest agent as the rest took positions to cover all angles of the surrounding area. "What took you so long?"

"Our apologies, Agent Harper. I'm Agent Harris, with Albatross unite Alpha. We are here to assist." Riley had almost forgotten the sound of her own name. She had lived as Alissa Lynn for so long, and committed even her thoughts to reflect that persona, that hearing her real name was a bit of a shock. "Once we had verified your location here in Panama, we had to slowly infiltrate the region.

Whatever powers that run this campus have ties in the country itself, making it incredibly difficult to get into the country, let alone this area. We had to take our time to make contact as the surround areas are tagged with booby traps and alarm systems."

"How long have you been in surveillance of the grounds?"

"For the better part of the past month and a half. The central building with the equipment on top is in constant contact with a satellite system that we couldn't hack. Until we had men on the ground, this region was impossible to watch from afar as it's protected by a no-fly zone and has some type of defense net keeping our drones from picking it up. We've made note of all vehicles leaving the facility, especially the larger groups, and have tracked any persons that have returned to the states."

"Returned? So that's where the so-called 'chosen' have gone. Why did you pick today to make contact with me?" Riley tried to keep her questions brief as she knew her time was limited.

"We confirmed that Samuel Stoke arrived in Panama last night." Riley could feel her heartbeat increase at the mention of Stoke's name. She had yearned for a second encounter with him since Nebraska. "We suspect that his arrival marks something significant in the campus operations as he is the only major player we've spotted in the vicinity of this place. He is currently in a small caravan enroute to this facility and should arrive within minutes."

"I need a weapon." Riley could see the look of hesitation on the agent's face.

"Director Locke specifically told me not to endanger your position here at the campus. I can't give you anything that would tip you off to the guards. Not to mention, you wouldn't be able to hide much in the garments you're wearing." Riley rolled her eyes.

"I am fully aware of the limitations of my apparel. I'm not asking for a gun. Give me a knife or something. If something's going down, I can't rely on your sharp-shooters to cover me in time." The agent sighed and removed a black blade from his belt. Riley grabbed it and tucked it into her waistband. "What's your plan of attack?"

"I have two sharp shooters in range to hit anything in the vicinity of the tower. I'll keep my men here in the woods as long as we can today, and if something happens, we'll storm the campus, but the first shots need to take out the dish on the roof of the tower. This will cut them off from satellites and other M.O.R.S. facilities, and we will also deploy a cellphone block in the area to eliminate all outside communication. We have handheld drones that can get up to the tower and begin downloading any digital traffic in case they try to corrupt their data."

"If something does happen, wait for my signal. Once the dish is down, you do what you need to do, but I need at least one man on me to go after Stoke."

"Understood, Agent Harper? Anything else to keep in mind? How should we treat the civilians?" Riley had to think for a moment.

"Obviously guards and facilitators should be considered combatants, but don't rule out the residents in white. They may not be the primary targets, but they could be in too deep and become fanatical. Watch your six when you're around them." The agent nodded and motioned for his men to recede back into the wilderness. Riley gave them one last look and then took off down the path.

****

As Riley returned to the main campus, she took care to calm her racing heart. Finally, the day had come where she could be herself once again. She kept her arms at her sides, trying her best to cover the outline of the knife in her pants. She had missed breakfast and could see all of the residents finding their yoga mats in the grass before the control tower. As she hurried over to the area, she noticed that someone had already taken the mat next to Margaret. Margaret mouthed that she was sorry, but Riley waved it off and took a mat on the other side of the green. As she sat down, she saw two tan SUVs enter the complex from the orchard road. The man that normally led communion went over to the lead vehicle and opened the door for none other than Samuel Stoke himself. Stoke shook the man's hand and walked with him over to the communion area.

"Ladies and Gentlemen, today is a special day. Our brother in the cause, Mr. Stoke, is here to join us in communion. We have filled your cups with his favorite communion wine, and as we partake, he is going to offer us a few words." As the residents bit into their piece of bread, and each swallowed their swig of wine, Riley quickly poured hers in the grass and ate her bread. From day one, Riley and Margaret had made it a point not to drink the communion wine. For Margaret it was a way to affirm her sobriety. In Riley's case, she simply didn't trust any liquid on campus other than the spring water. And that was a stretch in itself.

"Good morning folks, my name is Samuel. Now I know you have never met or heard of me, but that is because I am involved in other endeavors of M.O.R.S. Things are about to change, here in the world. You've all been taught that this world is in dire need of a change, or a cleansing. That's why you were brought here, to help prepare for that coming age. You may have noticed that some of your fellow believers have left this campus. They were chosen for missions elsewhere, but that doesn't mean you are any lesser than they."

Riley had her eyes pinned on Stoke. Thankfully she wasn't in the front rows, so he didn't seem to notice her. She now sported a dirty medium length cut as her red hair had grown out in the past few months. Though she was concentrating on every single word that Stoke uttered, she couldn't help but notice the strained breathing of the woman sitting next to her. Riley looked over to see the woman sweating profusely, eyes wide, and breathing short sporadic breaths.

"You have not been left behind, folks. No, instead you are going to be the first to move forward. Now I am sure you are beginning to notice that you are not able to move. The wine that you just drank had a certain sedative in it that has numbed your nervous system. We have told you about the Wrath of God, and the need to eradicate the evils within each of you. We are going to do that today, but I didn't want you to feel any pain." From behind the tall building, several guards emerged, Simon among them. Some of them held their normal rifle of choice, some held buckets and sticks with sponges, while others were equipped with flame throwers. "Normally we would all be destined to burn in the fires of hell, but not today! Today we will bask in the flame as we depart this world and go forth to another one. Each of you will be baptized and then released from this place! Do not worry, my friends. You will not feel a thing. You have earned you place here, and now it is time to leave."

To Riley's horror, Simon stepped forward with one of the buckets in hand, dunked his sponge in the bucket and then pressed the sponge down on the head of the person knelt before him at the end of the first row. Sitting two rows back, Riley could easily smell the stench of gasoline. She turned her head ever so slightly to look back at Margaret, knowing that she was likely the only other camper not affected by the paralyzing agent. Margaret had her eyes closed and a smile on her face as she seemed to be mouthing a silent prayer. By the time Simon made it to the end of his row, the first guard with the flamethrower stepped forward, pointed the firing tube, and pulled back on the trigger, engulfing the campers in flames. Riley fought against her instincts to spring into action, and instead she stayed frozen in place. The clearing was surrounded by guards, and she had no move to make. Stoke was burning people alive, and Riley could only wait for her turn.

Joshua D. Howell

3 SORRY, NOT SORRY

Riley braced herself for the screams, but there was nothing. If anything, she could only hear a faint humming as most of the campers were paralyzed enough that they couldn't make much of a noise. Riley watched as one by one, the bodies burned until they eventually slumped over on one another. Out of the corner of her eye, Riley could see Simon start down her row. Looking forward, Riley watched as Stoke took a handkerchief to cover his nose as he took his leave; escaping into the control tower, away from the stench. Suddenly, Riley's view was blocked as Simon stepped in front of her. Riley looked up at him and could see a sorrowful expression on his face.

"I'm sorry, Alissa. I was really rooting for you to be one of the ascended. I always liked you, you know." Simon crouched down and leaned forward to rub his thumb over Riley's cheek. He smiled at her for a moment before standing upright again and dunking his sponge in the bucket. "I'm sorry, Alissa. I really am."

"I'm not." Simon's expression turned to shock as Riley sprung forward, knife in hand, and dug the jagged blade deep into the man's thigh. Riley quickly sliced the knife upward until she felt it cut through Simon's femoral artery. As Simon began to fall, Riley rose and grabbed the bucket from his hand. Before the arsonist at the end of the row could make a move, Riley threw the bucket toward him; the wave of gasoline splashing over him, immediately catching fire.

"Hey!" Riley spun around to see one of the guards closest to her raise his rifle. Before he could get off a shot, however, Riley heard the zip of a bullet fly past her head to hit him just under his right eye. As he dropped, so did Riley. She quickly fumbled over Simon's blood soaked pants to release his sidearm from its holster. Simon grabbed her by the arm, his eyes pleading with her for help. She could tell by his grip that he had only moments left to live. Riley shrugged his hand away and rose to a bended knee position as she fired two rounds off into the nearest guard. More were closing in on her, but the flames from the rows ahead of her were blocking their sights. Riley fired a shot into the fuel tanks of a second arsonist, which caused a high-pitched hissing noise before the entire unit exploded and incinerated it's operator. Riley took out two more guards before she heard the scream from behind her.

"No! How could you?! You're ruining it, Alissa! You're ruining everything!" Riley turned to see Margaret running towards her with a small garden spade in her hand; she must have been tending to some of the plants before communion. Riley found herself standing and raising her hands up in protest, but she could see the look in Margaret's eyes and knew that it was worthless. Margaret may have never been named part of the "ascended," but she had whole-heartedly adopted this place as her new home. Riley may have lied to Margaret every day for the past six months, but that didn't mean that she had not developed even the basic feelings for her. She felt for Margaret's life of misguided decisions, and knew that this place was only the latest of Margaret's mistakes, but she was never in a position to truly attempt to help the poor girl; or at least that is what she had told herself in the dark of the barracks every night. Riley had known, all along, that this day would come, and had dreaded it.

Margaret made it within five feet of Riley, spade raised in her hand with tears on her cheek and a sorrowful betrayed expression across her face, before several bullets struck her in the chest. Riley watch as Margaret registered the pain, which caused her to trip and fall to the ground at Riley's feet. Riley turned to see one of the Albatross agents take position at her side as he verified his kill and then looked up to Riley, handing her an H&K G-36 assault rifle. Riley dropped to her knees, unfolded the stock, pulled back on the charging handle, flipped to switch to full-auto, and rose back to her feet to fire several rounds at the satellite dish on top of the control tower. After firing half of her 30 round magazine, the dish fell off its pedestal and crashed to the ground in pieces.

"We need to get to Stoke, now! Deploy the data drone!" The agent grabbed a handheld folded drone from his belt buckle, about the size of an old school Gameboy, and threw it up in the air. The drone came to life and began hovering above them.

"Drone in play!" The agent gave Riley an earpiece as they ran for the control tower entrance. Riley looked back at Margaret's lifeless body and allowed herself to mourn for her friend for a split second before putting in the earpiece and focusing on the chatter from the other team members.

"I've got control of the drone, downloading

now!"

"I've got eyes on Agent Harper and Agent Dritley, they're heading for the tower!"

"We've got incoming vehicles from the north and south gates!"

"Main campus is clear, take up defensive positions to engage the incoming forces!"

As Riley arrived at the secured door, she took position against the wall and looked for targets while Dritley set up charges on the door's hinges. Dritley tapped Riley on the shoulder twice and she quickly bent down and covered her head as the charges went off and blew open the door. Riley immediately bolted through the smoking entrance and down the industrial hallway toward the elevator on the far side. Riley could hear several guards broadcasting orders from an office halfway down the hallway.

"They've breached the main building! Get everyone here now! Our long range signal is blocked! We can't call headquarters for backup forces! Hurry!" Riley sprinted down the slick tiled hallway toward the guard station and quickly fell to her knees. Sliding along the floor past the open door, Riley raised her rifle, aimed into the guard station and sprayed several bullets into the nearest two guards before sliding out of view to the other side of the door. Riley slouched next to the wall and signaled Dritley to toss in a frag. Just as he did, a door further down the hall opened and Riley sprung to her feet. As the grenade exploded in the guard station behind her, Riley fired the rest of her first magazine down the hallway hitting the first of several guards emerging from the door.

As Riley closed the distance between herself and incoming guards, she dodged to her left, avoiding the bullets fired from one guard. She tossed her empty mag in his direction, hitting him in the face, then ran up one of the sides of the wall to her left and thrusted herself toward the nearest guard. Landing a downward superman punch, Riley brought the first guard to his knees as she dove under the rifle fire of the next guard. Dritley opened fire and put the one guard down as Riley took her knife and plunged it into the throat of the guard she had punched. The next guard closest to her landed his boot in her side, sending her stumbling backward. She threw her knife into his gut as she rolled on the floor and righted herself. Diving into the torso of the guard, she took the knife from his side and rammed it through his armpit while Dritley tackled the remaining guard to the ground and knocked him unconscious.

Rising to her feet, Riley pushed the button for

the elevator as Dritley handed her a second magazine for her G-36. Dritley took the elevator, as Riley opened the door and took the stairs. Scanning above for any guards above, Riley ascended the stairs and took position behind the third floor door. She waited for Dritley to catch up as listened to the on the other side side.

"Sir! Their coming up the elevator!"

"Well secure it you worthless imbeciles!"

The elevator arrived with a *ding!*, but Riley sprung through the stairwell door and opened fire on the three guards before the elevator doors could open. As the guards fell to the floor, Riley proceeded into a room, and Dritley dropped down from the ceiling of the elevator. The room behind the glass that had overlooked her communion and yoga sessions for months was basically a control base with several servers and terminals transmitting whatever data they were getting to a facility or facilities off site. As Riley entered, she locked eyes with Stoke and saw that he instantly recognized her.

"Oh, it's you." Stoke frowned, sighed and immediately turned his back to Riley. Pulling out his pistol, Stoke fired a round into the back of the head of the closest computer technician to him.

"Take him down!" Dritley ran and tackled Stoke like a linebacker taking out a quarterback. Riley advanced on the three people left over in the room, as they were clearly attempting to corrupt or delete the files that were stored on site. She shot the closest one in the foot. As the man fell from his chair and screamed out in agony, Riley aimed for the next person.

"I'll put holes in all of you if you don't back away from the keyboards now!" One technician immediately raised his hands, but a woman on the far side of the room quickly turned back to her station to type in some final commands. Riley took two steps forward and fired two rounds, hitting the woman in the neck and temple. As the woman slouched over in front of her bloodied monitor, Dritley looked up at Riley. Riley looked back at him and shrugged. "Hey, two alive out of three is good enough for me."

"We've got level 2 priority personnel on the third floor of the tower. I need a medic, and an extraction team for two." Dritley tossed Riley two pencil sized injectors. Riley popped the tops and tagged each of the remaining M.O.R.S. technicians in the neck. Almost immediately the two fell to the floor, unconscious. "Targets are sedated and awaiting detention."

"You got Stoke?" Riley looked out the window at the chaos. Bodies were still burning as the rest of the residents remained motionless in the midst of the gunfire. Several had been hit with stray bullets as more guards invaded the campus grounds and were met with fire from the Albatross Agents.

"Yep," Dritley said as he tightened the zip ties around Stoke's wrists and pulled him up. "What now?"

"Yes, indeed, what now Agent Harper?" Stoke smirked as he spit some blood on the carpet and looked back up at Riley. Riley grabbed the back of his head and kneed him across the face. As Stoke slumped over in an unconscious state, Riley looked back at Dritley.

"We're taking his ride."

4 MILK DOES THE BODY GOOD

Washington, D.C.

Congressman Jacob Tennison, from Ohio, was enjoying his late morning shower when he thought he heard a thud coming from somewhere in his condo. He popped his head out from the shower to listen, but heard nothing but the morning news crew on the television in the bedroom. Nonetheless, Tennison turned off the water, dried himself off with the towel, and donned his favorite white plush robe and slippers. Walking past his bedroom, Tennison descended the stairs at the end of the hallway and came to a stop at the living room. Nothing seemed out of order. He could see the shadow of one of the agents standing guard outside his door. Assuming he had been mistaken, Tennison headed for the kitchen.

Being a single man made for a lonely life in his

D.C. condo. While it allowed for the occasional one-night stand with a concerned constituent or a wayward street girl, it also made for a quiet home. The agents stood guard in the front and back, but he did not allow them inside. While he knew they could liven up his days in solace, he favored the status that dictated him higher than they. As he neared the kitchen, Tennison noted the smell of fresh coffee filling the hallway and immediately wondered if one of the assigned agents had summoned the arrogance to assume he could make some of his own. When Tennison reached the kitchen, however, he found that his assumptions were far from on the money.

All five of his assigned agents were on their knees in the middle of the kitchen; disarmed, gagged, and bound. Behind each agent stood a masked man with a trained rifle. The Congressman quickly turned to flee down the hall but found another man in a black tactical facemask standing behind him, blocking his path. Tennison was speechless as he backed slowly into the kitchen.

"Good morning, Congressman." Tennison almost jumped at the deep voice resonating from his left. He turned his head to see a figure in a black suit sitting at the dining table with a cup of coffee.

The figure rose and came into light. Tennison stumbled back in fear as he saw that the figure's head was nothing but a grinning beige skull. It took Tennison a few moments to compose himself, after he realized that the skull was merely a mask. "You can call me Mr. Bones. My apologies for frightening you sir, but I thought we might have ourselves a chat."

The skull-headed man kicked a stool over toward Tennison. Reluctantly, Tennison sat down on the stool while the gunman took a stance behind him, blocking any avenue to escape. He looked up into the black eye holes of Mr. Bones' skull, trying to find the eyes that hid within, but saw nothing but darkness. Mr. Bones smiled as he pulled a chair over from the dining room and placed it in front of Tennison. He sat down, backwards on the chair, and rested his arms on the back of the chair as he glared at the Congressman.

"What…uh. What do you want, Mr. Bones?" Mr. Bones raised his hand, which was covered in a glove that looked like a solid skeleton hand. He bent back all of his boney fingers but his index, which slowly pointed down at Tennison.

"Well, Congressman, I thought we would start by talking a little about your campaign funds." Tennison almost sighed, realizing this was all about money. He had plenty of money, and most of it was tucked away out of the purview of the I.R.S. While he would never admit to how much he had, he knew he could part with enough of it to get this freak show out of his home.

"My campaign funds! Of course, yes. You are probably referring to the off book figures. How much do you want?" Mr. Bones just stared at Tennison for a while, not moving or making a sound, before slowly looking to his right and nodding at one of his men. The man nodded back, pulled back the hammer of his assault rifle, raised it, and pulled the trigger. The full-automatic rifle sprung to life and fired a dozen rounds down into the back of the bound agent in a matter of seconds until the gunman released the trigger. The agent fell forward and hit the floor in a puddle of his own blood and innards. Mr. Bones slowly turned back to stare directly at Tennison. "Oh my God, why did you do that? I'll give you whatever you want! Just name it! Name it!"

"Information, Congressman. I want information. I already know about your nest eggs in the foreign banks. I don't care about how much money you stole from your constituents. I wanna talk about the money that you didn't keep for yourself. Specifically the two point four million dollars that you donated to Reynolds Pharmaceuticals." Tennison once again found himself speechless. How did this man know about those transactions? They were off the books, completely under the table, and went through shell corporations before they ever landed at Reynolds.

"I don't know…." Mr. Bones let out a sigh that cut off Tennison's mumbling. Bones turned his head again to the right, and the next gunman opened fire on the second bound agent. "For goodness sake, STOP! These men are innocent! They're part of the secret service! They know nothing!"

Mr. Bones rose from his chair and pulled it slowly across the floor back to the dining room; its legs screeching across the tile. Bones then pulled up the sleeves of his suit jacket as he walked over to the now deceased second agent lying on the floor. Bones rolled the body over and stuck his gloved hand under the bulletproof vest and fished around for a bit before pulling out the secret service badge. Bones held the bloodied badge up toward the light as he peered at it. He then bit down on the badge with his skeleton teeth before eventually looking up at Tennison, shrugging, and tossing the badge on the floor.

"It seems to me that these badges are store bought knockoffs. Which would mean that these men are privately hired, and I'm guessing they were supplied by the same organization that I'm inquiring about. Is that right?" Tennison sat in silence as Mr.

Bones stood over him. "But I can see you still have some sort of guilt over the deaths of these first two. So I'm going to give you the chance to spare the other three from the same, gory, gruesome fate as their comrades.

"I want you to tell me what your connection is with Reynold Pharmaceuticals and the organization known as M.O.R.S.?" Tennison couldn't help but choke a bit at the sound of the organization's name. No one knew that name. It was only just recently told to him, and he had nightmares about it every time he closed his eyes. "I want to know what the money is for, what you were promised, and who else on Capitol Hill is involved."

"I don't know, I swear it, I don't know. I'm just someone they squeezed for money in exchange for safe haven when it's all over."

"Safe Haven? From what?"

"I don't know, really, I don't!" Mr. Bones grabbed one of the rifles from his gunmen, kicked over the third bound agent, and sprayed him with several rounds of ammunition.

"Tell me, Congressman! Tell me now!"

"I don't know! I don't know!" Mr. Bones yelled out in anger as he fired the gun into the fourth and fifth agent, continuing to litter the fallen bodies with bullets until the magazine was out. Bones threw the rifle across the kitchen and stormed toward Tennison, grabbing him by the robe and shoving him against the refrigerator.

"You know something, Congressman, and I swear I will dismember you limb from limb, toenail from toe, every tooth from your damned mouth until you tell me what you know!" Bones threw the Congressman across the kitchen, cracking Tennison's head on the cabinet doors beneath the sink. Bones scanned the room until he found the knife block. He pulled out the first knife, a long knife, and gave it a look in the light before returning his gaze toward Tennison.

"Oh God, no! NO! I'll tell you what I know! I'll tell you!" Bones stepped toward Tennison, a firm grip around the handle of the knife. "Stop! Please! Stop! They told me they were going to take over everything! I thought they meant Congress at first, a hostile takeover, to secure their foothold, safe from any legislation that would hurt their business. But the money wasn't really for Reynolds, or pharmaceuticals at all. They told me it was going toward something bigger, something called M.O.R.S. And that if I was lucky, I could be among the survivors of whatever they were planning. I don't know what they are doing, or what the funds were really going toward. They never told me anything, so I assumed the worst! Noah's ark type shit! I was buying a ticket, that's all; safe passage!"

Mr. Bones stood over the Congressman with the knife in hand. His dark black eyes piercing Tennison's very being. Tennison didn't notice his own tears at first, but when he realized that he was crying in fear, he couldn't help but curl up into a ball beneath the looming figure. He covered his face with his hands, only peering enough through his fingers to watch the hand of Mr. Bones holding the knife. After a moment, the knife was lowered and Mr. Bones stepped back. After placing the knife back in its spot, Mr. Bones went to the fridge and grabbed the half gallon bottle of milk from it. As Tennison was helped to his feet by two of the gunmen, he watched as Mr. Bones took off the cap from the milk bottle and began to pour out the milk onto the kitchen island counter top and then the floor below.

"As disappointing as it is to hear, I believe you Congressman. So I'm not going to kill you." Tennison let out a big sigh. Whatever this was, it was going to be over. "Nope. Instead, I'm going to leave you to enjoy a nice glass of milk in your kitchen. Only you're going to accidentally spill your milk, then slip and bust your face on the nice marble counter top of your lovely kitchen island."

Before Tennison could beg or protest, the gunman to his left kicked his legs out from under him, while the gunman to his right grabbed the Congressman by the back of his hand and shoved it down. Tennison's face sunk into the edge of the marble counter, breaking every bone in his face and propelling them backward into his brain. His spinal column broke free from his head under all the pressure, as the Congressman's body fell limb against the kitchen island; his blood dripping down and to mix with the white puddle of 2% milk on the floor.

5 SLEDGEHAMMER

PANAMA

The Range Rover Sentinel drifted around the corner of the dirt road as Riley shifted gears and barreled down the road trying to put as much distance between her and the trailing M.O.R.S. vehicles behind her. She'd never driven a Sentinel before, but from what she could tell, it sure could take a beating. Having been t-boned by a jeep only moments earlier, as well as almost every panel shot to hell, she was fairly impressed with its durability. The bulletproof glass had taken the bulk of the damage, and it was still holding up quite well. Stoke was hogtied in the backseat, while Agent Dritley was firing outside the passenger window.

"I need a phone, Dritley."

"Not really the time, is it Agent Harper?"

"Did I ask your opinion, Agent?" Riley swerved to the left as another M.O.R.S. jeep sprung out from the tree line and onto the road. "Just give me a damn phone!"

Dritley pulled a satellite phone from his cargo pocket as he rolled up the window and reloaded his rifle. Riley watched as one of the jeeps began pulling up on her passenger side. Riley stepped on the brakes, pulled to the left and hit the gas. The front of Riley's Range Rover collided with the back right tire of the opposing Jeep and caused the vehicle to skid and twist until the body was being pushed by Riley's front bumper. Riley once again hit the brakes and pulled to the left, leaving the Jeep to continue skidding off the road and hug itself around a tree. As Dritley resumed firing on the remaining two vehicles behind them, Riley flipped over the satellite phone and dialed a number.

"This is Agent Riley Harper, SCID: alpha-five-tango-seven-seven." Riley waited for the line to switch to secure. "Put him on the phone, now!"

"This is Locke. Where are you Riley?"

"I'm on a country road outside the campus with Agent Dritley. We've got Stoke in custody, and are currently trying to lose two aggressive tails."

"We're pulling up Dritley's signal to get a GPS lock on you. I'll have an extraction point ready for you momentarily."

"No! No extraction. Not yet!" Riley saw a motorcycle coming up on her side. She hit the window button and shoved her G-36 out the window, spraying the motorcycle until it spun out of control and sent the driver flying. "I need a safehouse in Panama!"

"Absolutely not, Riley! We have protocols in place for this."

"I don't give a shit about protocol, Han! Get me a damn safehouse!" There was a pause on the other end, for a moment.

"I've sent the coordinates to Dritley's handheld. We'll notify the host that you're on the way. But you'll need to lose your tails first. But hear me, Riley! I want you to call in as soon as you're there. I will supervise your interactions via video."

"Fine." Riley hung up the phone and tossed in the glove box. She looked over at Dritley as he loaded the grenade launcher of his Berretta ARX 160. "You ready for this?"

Dritley nodded and he grabbed hold of the ceiling handle, as Riley pulled up on the parking brake and swung the Range Rover to the left in a hard U-turn. As soon as the SUV came to a halt, both Riley and Dritley had their doors open and began firing on the approaching vehicles through the opening between their doors and the vehicle cabin. Riley concentrated on the lead vehicle, hitting their windshield with as many shots as possible as Dritley launched the grenade toward the low end of the vehicles front bumper.

The projectile grenade made contact and exploded, obliterating the bottom half of the Jeep's engine as well as the front two tires, sending it flipping end over end. The vehicle behind it had little time to evade and ended up careening into the overturned heap of metal. Dritley tossed Riley his last grenade. After waiting for the doors to open on the second vehicle, Riley unclipped the grenade, and threw it to the ground near the open passenger door of the final Jeep. Riley fired off a few distraction shots until the grenade exploded, and then signaled Dritley to get back to their SUV. Once inside, Dritley pulled up the coordinates for the safehouse and Riley got the Rover back on the road.

****

EL CHORRILLO CORREGIMIENTO, PANAMA CITY

After a 30 minute race into the city, Riley finally pulled up to the address of the safe house. It resembled several of the other structures on the block; a two story, run-down apartment complex with graffiti covered walls, balconies, and holes in the building throughout. A man opened up a thin metal garage door and Riley drove the SUV in. Once inside, Riley saw the real building; a state of the art facility with every security measure one could imagine. The house host closed the thin metal door behind them, and then a second thick grade 3 impact resistant security door behind that.

Riley pulled Stoke's shirt over his head to cover his face as Dritley dragged his body from the vehicle. Riley got out of the car, rifle in hand, and motioned for the host to lead the way. He appeared young and fresh out of whatever training facility his agency had. She knew he wasn't an Albatross agent, and thus she couldn't allow him to see who their hostage was, or allow him out of her immediate sight.

"You CIA?" Riley figured she would control the conversation as the host led them down a steel walled hallway deeper into the complex. After passing a tech station with multiple screens full of camera angles from every inch of the outside perimeter, as well as an armory room that spiked Riley's interest, the host escorted Riley and crew to a second corridor.

"Yes, ma'am. My house is yours, I have some clothes for you here in the observation room down the hall. What else do you require?" The host opened a door to a secure interrogation room.

"I'd need a manifest of your inventory in order to answer that question." The host nodded and pulled a small tablet out of his back pocket. "I'm also going to need you to assist Dritley with setting up a video link from this room to a secure device at our headquarters. Once you've brought me what I need, I'll need you to take position somewhere else to watch the perimeter. I don't imagine we have much time."

"Were you followed?"

"No, but our enemy is incredibly resourceful." Riley scanned the tablet, highlighted several items, and returned it to the host. "Get me these asap, and then leave the tablet."

Dritley righted Stoke on a steel chair in the middle of the room and then proceeded to secure him. Stoke's hands were zip tied to the metal rods in the back of the chair and his ankles zip tied to the legs. After emptying Stoke's pockets and placing the items on the table, Dritley ripped open Stoke's silk shirt in order to attach heart monitor pads on certain parts of his chest. The pads were then linked to wires that Dritley plugged into a unit in the floor. As Dritley finished the setup, Riley quickly changed behind him. She dawned the pair of tactical pants, and pulled the t-shirt up and over herself. It felt good to where normal clothes again.

"We'll need to decrypt his phone and send whatever data we find to Locke. You'll need to be doing that while monitoring us from the tech room."

"Are you sure you don't want me in here with you?" Riley ignored Dritley's question as she passed a wand over Stoke's things and then over and around Stoke himself, looking for any tracking devices. When she found none, she signaled the host to lay the items she requested on the table; a toolkit, smelling salts, a couple water bottles, a power drill, an M-9 pistol, and the tablet. "Thank you. Now, go set up that video link with Dritley."

As Riley waited for the good ahead, she leaned against the table and stared down at Stoke. For the past 6 months, playing a weak minded hitchhiker and hanging out at the camp for misfits, she had only thought of this man. She swore that she would avenge Peter, and now she stood before the man that killed him. She could easily kill him, but then Albatross would have next to nothing. While Riley was certain some kind of information was recovered from the morning's raid, Stoke would be able to give her some gold. He was, in fact, the "S" in "M.O.R.S." The speaker in the far corner crackled a bit as it came on.

"I'm here Riley. You may begin." Locke's voice sounded tense. It was clear to Riley that her boss was not onboard with this situation, but he wasn't in Panama, and thus he couldn't stop her.

"Thanks dad." Riley popped a packet of smelling salts under Stoke's nose and watched as he pulled back his head and came to life. Riley tossed the packet, leaned in, and slapped Stoke a couple times on his left cheek. "Ok Samuel, time to wake up."

"Huh? Where am I?"

"You're in my home, Samuel. You're on my turf, now." Samuel looked around the room, and after a moment began to smile.

"Oh you've done it now, Agent Harper. You

finally plucked the last straw, and I dare say that you are about to reap your reward, I promise you that." Stoke leaned to his right and spit on the floor. He took a moment to look up, directly into the camera, winked, and then turned back to Riley. "You better get on with it darling, because they've seen my face now."

"Why are you in Panama? What about today forced your hand?" Riley looked up at the camera, wondering what he meant about 'them' seeing his face. The video was being transmitted over a secure link. Either way, she felt an unnerving need to rush.

"That's what you're starting with, Red?" Stoke laughed a bit before clearing his throat. "I don't even have to make something up for that. We were cutting our loose ends, that's all. All things end in time."

"Where did the 'chosen' ones go?"

"Ah, see now that's the right question. Wouldn't you like to know." Riley backhanded Stoke across the face. "There it is. I was wondering how long it would take to get your hands on me."

"Answer the question." Stoke leaned forward, as much as he could with his restraints and looked Riley in the eye.

"Why? What possible reason would I have to tell you a damn thing?" Riley looked up at the camera. The speaker popped on.

"You're cleared for level 3." Locke kept it short and sweet, but told Riley what she needed to hear. It was pre-established that interrogations through Albatross had 5 levels of pain. Each level required permission from a supervisor. Level 5 was on par with Riley's slap, while Level 1 was closer to waterboarding and strangulation. Level 3 was a nice medium, but it wasn't enough for Riley.

"Oh who's that? Is that your slimy Korean boss? I didn't know he was watching." Stoke looked back up at the camera. "Hey Han! How have you been? We've been looking for you and your little band of misfits."

Riley turned around to the table and opened the tool box. There were so many small items that could generate immense amounts of pain, but Riley was leaning towards something with a little less finesse. She decided on the 20lb sledge hammer. It felt good in her hands, and she enjoyed the weight. Turning around, she locked eyes with Stoke.

"Samuel. You're done. It's time to end this desperate performance of yours and tell me what I want to know. You're going to answer my questions, or I'm going to use this." Stoke's expression didn't change, but his eyes flickered a bit.

"Really? What is this, amateur hour? You threaten to bash my head in if I don't tell you things? That seems incredibly unproductive." Stoke turned back to the camera. "Wow, Han, who the hell does your recruiting?"

"Fine." Riley lifted the hammer back above her right shoulder, and swung like it was her opening drive of an 18 hole tournament. The hammer's head collided with Stoke's right knee, dislocating and cracking it severely. Stoke screamed out in pain.

"Riley!" Locke's voice filled the room. He clearly wasn't happy. Riley dropped the hammer and grabbed a needle from the table. She slammed it down into Stoke's thigh as Stoke openly sobbed in agony.

"Now I've just injected you with a special concoction that will keep you awake and lucid until I'm done with you. As you can tell, it's not numbing any of your pain, but it's going to keep you from passing out on me. So we are going to play this game where I break something of yours until tell me what I want to know!"

"You stupid bitch!" Riley picked up the sledge

hammer and brought it slamming straight down on the same knee. Stoke shrieked in utter anguish.

"Dammit Riley! Stop it now!" Riley held up a middle finger to the camera, but didn't take her eyes off Stoke. Locke could punish her all he wanted when she got back, but in this moment, he couldn't do a thing to her.

"Probably not the time to insult me, Sam. That knee looks like some soggy mashed potatoes right about now. I think I'll aim for your ankle next." Riley dropped the hammer and slapped Stoke across the face. "Now I'll be more than happy to kill you, Sammy, after that shit you pulled with Peter, but I don't just want you. I want all of M.O.R.S. I know what the letters mean, but I need to know who's who. You're the 'S,' and the late Jane Reynolds is the 'R'. Who are the other two?"

"I don't know," Stoke snarled under his breath.

"Oh for goodness sake, Sam. Am I going to have to take your whole damn leg?" Riley reached for the sledge hammer, but Stoke jerked forward in his chair.

"I said I don't know! I never knew! I only met with Jane. We all only met with Jane! She ran things in the beginning and left instructions to follow in her absence. We never knew each other, only that we all represented the top tier in our respected fields."

"What fields?"

"Oh come on! Am I going to have to spell it out for you?" Riley took a knife and jabbed it down into Stoke's right leg, making sure to avoid anything fatal. Stoke's jaw dropped as Riley twisted the knife and watched as the pain rippled across Stoke's face. "Please! You barbaric wench! Stop!"

"I'll stop when you deliver!"

"Major Industries! The ones that run the world! Agriculture, weaponry, human genetics and pharmaceuticals, oil! Control those, and you can make your desires become a reality."

"What's the next phase of your operation? Why dismantle the Church of MORS?"

"You'll find out soon."

"Are you trying to buy time? Is that it?" Riley picked up the M9 and pressed against Stoke's forehead. "Your friends aren't coming. Even if they are, you can be damned sure you won't make it out of here alive."

"Do you....*sigh*...Do you know who I am?" Stoke

smiled his bloody teeth up at Riley, before narrowing his lips and glaring at her; his pain now turned to rage. "DO YOU KNOW WHO I AM? I am not some whore you can buy! I don't give freebies, and you can't match what M.O.R.S. is giving. So you can either pull the trigger, or back the hell off!

Riley stepped back, releasing pistol from Stoke's forehead, leaving a slight circular indentation of the barrel on Stoke's skin. She took a breath and stared down at Stoke as he caught his breath and returned her stare. After a few moments, Stoke began chuckling in between his wincing.

"I heard it was you that put him down; our mutual friend, Peter the police officer." Riley tightened her grip on the handle of the gun. "I was hoping he would change quick enough to take out a few of your friends, but it seems he had slightly more strength than I anticipated and was able to hold it back a little longer. Did he beg for mercy, Agent Harper? Did he whimper like a bitch, like he did when my men operated on him?"

"Agh!" Riley screamed as she flipped the handgun over, grabbed it by the barrel, and struck Samuel across the back with the grip of the gun; breaking Stoke's nose and forcing him to turn his face to the side and spew chunks of blood and cartilage. Riley grabbed Stoke by the jaw, brought his face back to her and punched it, then again with her other hand, and again, and again, left and right, all the while screaming at him. Finally, she punched him hard enough that Stoke, and the chair, fell back and over to one side. Riley stood there, looking at Stoke's helpless state. "Look at you, and you're bludgeoned face, bleeding all over my floor. No one gives a damn about you, Samuel. No one will herald you as some great scientific mind of our time. No one will know your name."

"No, ugh, they won't. Much to my distain, of course." Stoke spit out a glob of blood across the hard floor as his face clung to the cement. He watched as his blood began to trickle into a stream that found its way to a drain in the center of the room. He strained to look up at Riley, but could only move his eyes. "They won't know my name, but by the end of today, the world will know the name of M.O.R.S."

"What? Today? Why today?" Riley grabbed Stoke's chair and righted it. She repeated her question, but Stoke only coughed and laughed. She grabbed his face in her hand and demanded an answer, but Stoke could only force a broken bloody smile. Before Riley could do anything else, a loud *BOOM!* shook the building. The speaker crackled on again.

"Agent Harper! We've been breached!"

Riley cocked her M9, and went to the door. She turned back to Stoke. She could kill him then and there; clean shot to the back of the head. She nearly raised the gun in his direction, but stopped herself. She needed more than just the satisfaction of killing him. She opened the door, walked through the observation room to the hallway door, and slowly opened it.

The hallway was engulfed in smoke. The echoing of gunfire was deafening. Agent Dritley must have had time to bunker himself in, because it sounded like he was putting up quite a fight. Riley contemplated going to help him, but she couldn't leave her prisoner. Suddenly the firing stopped, but was quickly followed by the sound of boots on the hard floor. The rest of Albatross team had not been informed of the safe house location, so Riley could only assume that Dritley had fallen.

She quickly shut the door and locked it; both the electronic and hard lock. She quickly grabbed one of the metal chairs in the observation room and shoved it under the door handle. Retreating back into the interrogation room, Riley grabbed the table and pulled up the building specs. She knew, at this point, that she couldn't keep Stoke captive, and that her first priority was to avoid being captured herself. Safehouses are designed for evasion upon being breached, and so Riley hoped there was a way out of her current predicament. To her relief, she found a solution.

According to the tablet, there was a false wall in the southeast corner of the room. The panel was just large enough for a person to crouch through. Riley turned back to Stoke and looked him in the eyes, her gun raised. Stoke smiled back at her, almost inviting her to pull the trigger. Just before she did, another explosion erupted as the observation room was breached. In the seconds before the smoke and dust settled, Riley bent down and pushed through the false wall. The panel was thick, like the security doors in the oval office, and sealed and locked behind her. Once inside and secure, Riley stayed put as she pulled up the cameras and watched as Stoke was rescued.

The rescue crew was made up of 10 soldiers in black, led by a woman with long, blonde hair. The woman was outfitted in protective gear and wore a face shield. The audio was out, but Riley could tell that Stoke was saying something to the effect of "she's in the walls!" Riley knelt down and covered her head as the soldiers in the room quickly turned and opened fire at the wall. Once the soldiers realized that the walls were sufficient enough to hold up to their bullets, the woman motioned to one of them to put up explosives before turning to leave the room.

Riley opened a hatch and dropped down the attached ladder. Reaching up, Riley quickly closed the hatch behind her and locked it before sliding down the ladder to the tunnel below. As the lights flickered on, Riley heard the *BOOM* above her. She ran down the hall to a makeshift underground garage. There was an additional armory behind a metal cage. Once inside, Riley threw on a bulletproof vest, grabbed a backpack, and stuffed it with as many useful items as she could find while keeping an eye on the camera feeds she had streaming on the tablet. She grabbed a Sig MPX Mini off the wall and found the extended magazines for it and stuffed them in the straps of her vest. The MPX was basically a handheld mini machine gun that could fire with fair accuracy while operating a vehicle. She looked again to the tablet and knew she only had a few moments before the rescue crew decided to stop searching for her and leave with their prize.

The wall of the interrogation room must have been reinforced with something, because Riley heard no attempts to open the hatch. She quickly exited the cage and threw her bag of gear over to the motorcycle. She ran to the operations desk and grabbed one of the black boxes stacked along the side. As in most safe houses, this one was prepped in case of an attack. The secret tunnel, the 2nd armory, and this electronics desk were there for this very purpose. Inside the box was a mini sat phone, ear piece, and a smart phone sized GPS unit.

The GPS unit fit exactly in a small space on the top of the Zero Stealthfighter motorcycle. After typing in her credentials, the unit turned on the electric bike and gave her a GPS street view with intersection data, police bandwidth monitoring and the basic route guidance a normal GPS would have. Riley dialed up the Sat phone, connected it with her ear piece, and waited for Locke to come on the line.

"Are you alright?" Locke had a genuine tone of concern.

"I'm fine, but I'm alone. Dritley is down and I'm sure the host is as well." Riley heard another deafening **BOOM** above her, this one more significant as dust and small pieces of debris started falling around her. "You were watching. Stoke told us this was going to happen. Who has access to our feeds?"

"We're looking into it, Riley, but right now you

need to go. They just incinerated the building and your bunker tunnel won't hold out much longer." Riley revved the throttle a bit as she checked the gauges; all looked good.

"I've got street maps here, but I could use your eye in the sky to keep track of their convoy."

"I'd advise you not to follow, but I doubt you'd obey."

"Listen if it was as simple as tracking their movements, we'd have them by now. We'd have them all, Han. If they can see our transmissions, they can take over whatever satellites we are using. If they get to a plane, they are gone. Clearly they have the power to stay off the radar." Riley donned the backpack, and tightened the straps. She clipped the Sig into the side gun mount on the motorcycle, pulled on a pair of gloves, and put on the bulletproof helmet. "Now give me your help, or put someone on the line that will."

6 THERE GOES THE FREEWAY

Riley shifted into gear and released the clutch as the bike sprung forward down the narrow underground tunnel. As she passed a sensor in the wall, lights at the end of the tunnel popped on to reveal a ramp that lead to a small door opening in the ceiling. The bike accelerated up the ramp and leapt out into the air of a back alley behind the burning safehouse building.

"Take the alley down two blocks and take a left." Locke had apparently decided to help her, and Riley wasn't going to deny it. She accelerated down the alley, across the street and down the next alley before turning left and joining the traffic flowing toward the city. Riley stood up on the motorcycle a bit to see above the cars. She saw two black SUVs rushing back and forth between lanes about a block ahead of her.

"I see them." Riley pulled back on the throttle and jetted down the street, weaving between the cars to close the gap between herself and the SUVs.

"I'll remind you that you're surrounded by civilians, Agent. Civilians that can easily become collateral damage should you open fire. You're personal connection with Stoke is clouding your judgement. You've been out of the game now for several months. You haven't been training. You need to think this through."

"Stop treating me like a child, Han! I know how to fire a damn weapon. Now watch my six and shut the hell up."

****

In the armored SUV, Samuel Stoke sat curled up in a sweaty mess in the back seat. While he was writhing in pain, he was lucid enough to realize the situation he was in. He had been rescued, yes, but he had been rescued by HER. If it had been a no name, no faced agent he would have assumed business was as usual, but that was clearly not the case. The woman sitting on the other side of the SUV was not known to step out from the keep to perform a mission. It was not because she was afraid to get her hands dirty, though, as it normally meant that if she was present, she was going to get those hands incredibly dirty. Knowing this, Stoke was uncertain whether he was sweating because of the pain, the heat, or the fear of his current predicament.

"You were sloppy, Samuel." The woman didn't turn to face him, but stared out the window while she removed her black gloves.

"Yes, ma'am, I was, but I swear I…" but Samuel's plead was cut short by the woman raising her hand to silence him.

"You know damn well you didn't need to be down here for the cleanup, but your lust for destruction got the better of you, and put us all at risk." The woman leaned forward, reached behind her back and pulled out a 9 millimeter handgun from its back holster. Placing the gun on her lap, the woman turned to Stoke. "The fact that you're still conscious and sweating as profusely as you are tells me that you were given a cocktail of some sorts while in that bunker. I think it would be a fair guess to assume that a truth serum was among the ingredients, and so I'm going to use that to my advantage. Now I want you to tell me what you said to Agent Harper."

"Ma'am!" The screen between the driver's seat

and the back seats rolled down just before Samuel opened his mouth. The man in a black tactical outfit looked back as he cocked his rifle. "We have a tail fast approaching from the rear."

"Does this bitch not know when to give up?!" The woman looked back through the glass to see Agent Harper swerving between cars on a motorcycle, quickly closing the distance. While the woman was impressed with Harper's ability to stay alive, she was more than annoyed at this point. "Put two and three in motion, without restraint. If she wants to piss me off, she's going to have to face the consequences. Tell the pilot to get preparations underway. I want to be in the air within 5 minutes of our arrival."

****

Riley could see the black SUV about 10 cars in front of her. Traffic was keeping a steady pace while also staying fairly congested as the highway led around the city toward the airport. She tried to close the gap by riding the lane dividers between cars, but could only go so far before one car swerved between lanes and cut her off. They had to see her at this point, but she didn't care. Stoke was not leaving her sight.

"Harper, you've got two incoming vehicles from

behind."

Riley looked back to see two more black SUVs speeding up the shoulders of either side of the highway. Within moments they had passed her and began forcing their way across lanes to position themselves between Riley and Stoke's vehicle. Riley was surprised it took them this long to show up, as she reached down and grabbed her MPX from its mount on the side of the bike. The trunk of the SUV on the right began to slowly lift up revealing, to Riley's horror, a man crouched behind a mounted M134 six-barrel rotary machine gun. Riley slammed on the breaks as the man pulled the trigger and began obliterating everything in its path.

Riley watched as the fiery stream of bullets made its way across the lanes of traffic. Cars began to swerve out of the way as the bullets cut through them like butter. As the shooter rotated the minigun toward Riley, she watched in revulsion as a woman in the car next to her was cut to pieces, splattering the windows in dark red, and causing the car to swerve and hit the cars on either side. Riley continued to break until she was a few car lengths back and out of range of the minigun, hoping the shooter would cease fire.

"Dammit! Locke, they've got some massive

firepower and they don't care about collateral damage. What's the play here?" Riley swerved between cars as they crashed into each other, trying to keep her speed high enough not to lose the black caravan ahead of her.

"I told you to let them go, Riley! Local police have been notified, and we've sent word to have men on the ground at the airport. You need to pull back." Riley knew he was right as she slowly released the throttle. The minigun had stopped firing, and she didn't need to endanger any more civilians. Unfortunately, the backup SUVs seemed to be also slowing down; they appeared to want to finish this. With no civilians following the SUVs, Riley had a vacant stretch of highway that she could pursue if she cared to. The SUVs seem to have stopped about 100 yards away, waiting for her to make her move. Riley decided not to disappoint them.

"They've given me a window, Locke. I'm taking it." Riley revved up the bike and navigated around the remaining cars in front of her until she was in the clear. As the SUV on the left opened its trunk to expose two men aiming assault rifles at her, Riley knew her options were limited. The men opened fire, and soon the minigun in the other SUV started whirring up again. Patches of concrete began to explode as the line of fire tried to catch up to Riley.

Riley swerved back and forth across the 4 lane highway, evading what fire she could while aiming her MPX and returning fire. At this speed and amount of veering back and forth, Riley's aim was fairly worthless, but she was forcing the two men on the left to take cover. Riley kept swinging back and forth, ducking and diving out of the way of the minigun's rapid string of bullets. Thankfully, the speed of her bike was fast enough to stay ahead of the stream of fire as she focused on outrunning her demise.

She could see Stoke's SUV continuing on in the distance, and realized that she needed to bypass this obstacle and get back to her pursuit. Riley slid her weapon back into its mount and reached back into her backpack for a grenade. The specialty frag had a digital time and a push button top to activate. Riley slid her thumb to the timer arrow and pressed it 5 times as she kept her eye on the mini gun. Passing under its stream of fire Riley swung out to the far right wall of the highway as she took the bike into high gear. Riley pressed down on the pressure activate top button as she neared the minigun vehicle.

1….

The stream of nonstop bullets closed in on Riley

from her left as she reached top speed.

2....

Riley swerved left, hugging the body of her bike as tightly as possible as she ducked down under the barrage of bullets.

3....

As she continued to swing wide left to avoid fire from the two assault rifles, Riley gauged the gap between the two parked SUVs.

4....

Riley quickly veered into the middle lane and sped between the SUVs, tossing the grenade into the back of the SUV with the minigun just as she passed.

5....

Bracing herself for the detonation, Riley hoped she could clear the blast in time. The SUV exploded behind her in a fantastic burst of fire pushing the other SUV over onto its side. Riley exhaled and grinned, amazed at her own luck. She could still see the remaining SUV in the distance, about a half mile up the road as she attempted to accelerate a bit more to catch up.

****

"I didn't give her anything actionable, I swear." If Samuel Stoke's knee wasn't in pieces, he would have attempted to kneel in the back of the SUV.

"You implied enough, Stoke! I am sick of excusing you for your arrogance!" The woman cocked the handgun and aimed it toward Stoke. In that moment, Stoke realized that groveling wasn't going to work.

"I'm calling your bluff. You think that M.O.R.S. can survive without me? There's still so much work that needs to be done, and I'm the only one with the brains to pull it off!" Stoke gritted his teeth through the pain as his anger began to foam up in his mouth. "So knock off the scare tactics and get me to a fricking hospital!"

"I'll admit it, you've always had the balls to make it in this business," The woman pulled back on the trigger and fired a single round between the eyes of Mr. Stoke, coating the window behind him with his insides. "but your brains, while intriguing, were never irreplaceable."

****

Closing in on Stoke's SUV, Riley once again reached for her MPX. Just as she was about to begin firing on the back of the vehicle, however, Riley saw the passenger side door open and watched as a body was pushed out into the air. Riley swerved to avoid the bloodied heap as it bounced and rolled down the road. In the seconds that she passed it, Riley looked down to recognize Stoke's face and see the bullet hole in his forehead. In confusion, Riley looked back up to see the woman reach out and pull the door shut.

"Locke! They just killed Stoke!"

"I saw it, Harper. You've got a police vehicle coming up behind you. Continue tailing the vehicle along with the police until we can apprehend them at the airport."

Riley secured the MPX back into its mount and slowed down a bit, allowing the cop car to catch up to her. The car came up on her right and matched her speed. The police officer signaled for Riley to second him in pursuit, and she nodded as the car kicked-in its turbo and accelerated forward. Suddenly, the car came to a halt and turned to the left to block Riley's path. Riley hit the brakes hard, her back tire rising off the pavement, but it wasn't enough to avoid the impact.

Riley's front wheel hit the front half of the cop car and sent her flying over the hood and onto the concrete on the other side. Riley rolled to a stop and squirmed in pain as she fought to stay awake. She could hear Locke calling out to her over the earpiece, but it sounded like he was a mile away. She saw the cop exit his vehicle and run to her side. He picked her off the ground and began walking her further down the road, away from his vehicle. Riley turned her head in pain as she realized where he was taking her. In her last moments of consciousness, Riley saw the black SUV come to a stop and its driver jumping out to open the trunk. Just before the darkness overtook her, Riley saw the trunk close and heard the woman in the backseat tell the driver to go.

7 HELLO THERE

ALBATROSS UNIT

"What the hell happened out there, Locke?" Eugene's voice carried through the command center as he made his way past the rows of computers towards Locke's office.

"Mr. Pierce, good of you to show up to work today." Locke turned and walked into his office as Eugene ascended the stairs, hot on Locke's heels

"Can the shit! I saw the feed. How could you let this happen? First you allow Riley to pursue the caravan, knowing damn well that she has been out of the game for 6 months, then she gets grabbed, and finally… your men failed to secure the damn airport!" The doors closed behind Eugene, sealing them in, though Locke wondered if the soundproof glass was of a high enough grade to keep Eugene's voice from resonating throughout the bunker. "Tell me you're tracking the damn plane, Locke! Tell me you didn't just lose our Agent who's been out in the wild for the last six fricking months!"

"We lost the plane twenty minutes ago. M.O.R.S. has access to satellites, and so it is safe to assume that they were able to ghost the jet on its way back to the States. We are monitoring as many receiving airports as we can for incoming flights." Eugene kicked a chair over. "We'll find her, Eugene. I promise we will. Right now we can only wait for the plane to show up, as well as process whatever we can from the cult grounds."

"You better have found something, Locke. Or the last six months will be have been for nothing!" Eugene slammed his hands down on Locke's desk and leaned in. Locke slowly rose from his chair and leaned in to meet Eugene face to face.

"You only get so many of these little outbursts. I wouldn't press your luck much further than you currently have, Mr. Pierce." Eugene met Locke's stare, but eventually broke his glare and stepped back from the desk. "Thank you. I appreciate your compassion, but I made it clear when I brought you onto this team, that you would have to bend to my command while serving in the Albatross Unit. Don't forget the pledge you made."

"I haven't." Eugene picked up the chair and put it back in place. He took a seat and slouched forward. "Just give me something to do. I can't sit still right now."

"I've got men and women combing through the data we recovered. I called out to our mutual friend, Ms. Cubro, to drop by today to go over some of the locations and see if there's any sites that we can make a move on. Meanwhile, our people are trying to determine what Samuel Stoke meant when he said the world would know the name M.O.R.S. by the end of today."

"How many of the 'ascended' cult members that returned over the last six month do you still have eyes on? They have to be linked somehow." Locke turned in his chair and clicked his remote. A map of the United States was projected onto the wall behind his desk. Several red dots were spread over the map.

"We currently have Agents tailing a few dozen of them. We lost track of many of them once they got back across the border. Most of them didn't have missing persons records, and many of them never returned home either. Without a list of names, it wasn't exactly easy to determine which were cult members and which were your average American returning home from a vacation. Those that we know about for sure haven't shown any abnormal activity in the past couple days, at least none that has been reported back from their tails. I've sent out emergency messages to keep our people on high alert."

****

OMAHA, NEBRASKA

Agent Navarro walked up to the side of the black Crown Vic with a coffee in each hand. Placing the coffees on the roof, he reached down to open the door, and grab the pack of cigarettes that had fallen out of his pocket and on to the floor of the car. He took a moment to lean on the side of the car and enjoy a smoke. It was a sunny, gorgeous day in the city, and nothing felt more right to him than taking it all in with a cig in between his fingers. That is, of course, unless one were to also combine it with some of the signature coffee that he loved to get at Legend Comics. Back when he had more free time, Navarro used to hit up this little hole in the wall comic shop in an old strip mall off Leavenworth Street. Since then, he got a promotion and moved up in the world, and so did the comic shop.

Now it was known as Legend Comics and Coffee, and had moved up the street into an antique brick building where their products could be showcased like the works of art they were. Aside from his favorite picture books, the joint now sold coffee that was unmatched in flavor, in his opinion. Since their stake out point was just down the street from Legend Comics and Coffee, Navarro took the opportunity to get his favorite cup of joe every morning. As he took the first sip and breathed in the morning air, he almost couldn't hear his partner's voice, yelling at him to get his ass in the car.

"Give me my damn coffee before it gets cold, ya selfish bastard." Agent Jacobs sat leaning over the steering wheel, trying to find the right angle that would keep the sun blocked by the overhanging tree's branches. Navarro plopped down next to him and handed him the coffee. "Finally! I swear you spend more time looking at those comics than retrieving the coffee every morning."

"I nearly jogged back here, you dick." Navarro kept one leg outside of the car as he took another pull from his cigarette. "Just be grateful, man."

"Don't give me that crap. Now get your butt in the car and put out that cig. We're supposed to be keeping a low profile." Navarro rolled his eyes and flicked the cigarette as he shut the door and laid back in his now reclined seat. "And don't get too comfortable. I need you alert, Navarro. We just got a text to be on the lookout."

"Oh be on the lookout for what? We've been watching this broad for two months and have come up with nothing short of nothing, man! I mean what time is it, like 11:30 a.m.? I guarantee you she's in there watching her morning soaps while she finishes her fourth batch of sugar cookies for the school's bake sale on Thursday. In fact in the next 15 minutes, Mrs. Janice Griffin is going to drive downtown to either catch lunch with her fellow fundraiser moms or with her Aunt Sherrie. You know how I know this, Jacobs?" Jacobs grunted and rolled his eyes. "Because it's happened every single freaking day we've been here! Every day! Fricking clockwork, man. Boring-ass clockwork."

As if to solidify Navarro's claims, the side door of the yellow house half way down the street suddenly opened and out came Janice with a long coat on and her purse in hand. From what Navarro could tell, Janice was wearing her baggy workout sweats, which only seemed to annoy him that his predictions didn't seem to match her lethargic style of the day. Still, he was right about her leaving for lunch, and found contentment in that as he brought up his chair and put on his seatbelt. As Janice pulled out of her driveway and made her way down the block, Jacobs started the car and began to follow.

"You'd think we could have landed a better vehicle than this heap of crap."

"Oh for the love of goodness, do you ever shut up Navarro?" Jacobs took a swig of his coffee as he turned onto Center street and continued to follow Janice as she headed toward downtown. "Besides, Crown Vics are as sturdy and reliable as they come in terms of quality vehicles."

"Yea, for cop cars! We might as well just have a sign up top that says HEY, WE'RE THE FEDS!" Navarro watched as Janice switched lanes and popped her turning signal as she crossed over and into the parking lot of the Beals Elementary School.

"Ha! Guess your prediction was wrong, buddy. Looks like she's picking up little Tiffany for lunch today." Navarro shrugged and drank his coffee as they pulled over to the curb down the street.

"Yea well she ain't dressed for it."

"Wow. Maybe you have been on this gig for too long if you're starting to judge her daily outfits." Jacob laughed, but Navarro just stared out the window. He watched as Janice shuffled her way into the school, and then returned outside moments later with little Tiffany in tow.

Janice didn't necessarily seem to be rushing, but she did seem to have a specific pace that Navarro took note of. He saw the way she took little Tiffany to the car, her hand on Tiffany's back, keeping the pace, instead of holding her hand. Navarro grabbed the log book and began looking over the past couple weeks.

"Does Tiffany have an appointment today? Doctor? Dentist? Anything?" Navarro continued to search through the text, now looking at the transcripts of recent phone calls made from the Griffin residence.

"Uh, no. I don't think so. Why you think Janice is taking her somewhere? She doesn't seem flustered." Jacobs turned over the engine as Janice's car re-entered the street and returned to making its way toward downtown.

"No, she doesn't look flustered. But she doesn't look determined. She's got an appointment of some kind, Jacobs. Keep on her tail." Navarro rifled through the bank statements they had acquired, looking for plane or bus tickets, but found none. Still, she was heading downtown and it wasn't normal for her to take her daughter out of school without a scheduled appointment.

After a few minutes of following at a safe distance, Agents Navarro and Jacobs watched as Janice's car came to a stop on the curb outside of the Woodman Tower building. Navarro knew this building well. When he was a young assistant in the county courthouse across the street, he used to skip over to the Woodman to drop off his paychecks at the bank on the bottom floor, or slip up the midlevel to get something from their cafeteria. The Woodman used to be the tallest building in Omaha, and even had a rotating restaurant on the top floor. That was before Navarro's time, but he remembered hearing his parents talk about it.

"This is her bank right?" Navarro looked back at the bank records.

"Yep this is it. Pull over behind this car, I might need to get out." Jacobs pulled into a spot a few cars back from Janice's car.

"Hold your horses, kid. We stay in the car unless there's cause not to." The two agents watched as Janice exited the vehicle. "Although I will give you that, sweats and that long coat. She's definitely not trying to impress anyone today."

Navarro ignored the comment and watched Janice as she came around to the passenger side and opened the door for Tiffany. The sidewalk was getting a bit crowded as the masses seemed to be taking their lunch all at the same time. As Navarro tried to focus past the passersby, he saw Janice crouch down and chat with Tiffany. They seemed to be laughing as Janice adjusted Tiffany's dress and played with the child's hair. They embraced in a hug, and Navarro couldn't help but smile at the sight; a truly loving mother was all that he could see. Perhaps she was having a rough day and simply wanted to take her daughter on some mid-day errands.

Perhaps she had planned to withdraw some cash and hit up the ice cream joint down the street for a middle of the day treat. Navarro took another sip of his coffee and then attempted to put it down, for he couldn't find the cup holder slot without physically looking down to guide his hand to it. Looking back up, Navarro gazed through the crowd of people walking up and down the block until he found them again. Navarro popped up in his seat as he realized that little Tiffany was now standing alone on the sidewalk with Janice nowhere to be found.

"Shit, where'd she go, Jacobs?." Jacobs had clearly been distracted as he was now leaning forward and searching the crowd just as Navarro was. "I'm going."

Navarro unbuckled his seatbelt and jumped out of the car, making his way through the lunch crowd on the sidewalk. He tried to break into a slight jog, but the area had become so congested that he could only get to a brisk walk. Finally, he reached Tiffany and found her still standing there, alone, now crying to herself. Navarro plopped down next to the ten year old and pulled out his badge.

"Hello there, Miss. My name's Miguel and I'm police officer. Are you alright?" Tiffany was clearly a bit shy as she stepped back from Navarro. He quickly scanned the area, looking for Janice, but couldn't see her. He returned his attention back to Tiffany and hoped that she could help. "Where's your mommy, little girl? Is she around somewhere?"

"She told me she loved me, but that she had to go away!" Tiffany was now bawling with tears as she blurted out her sentence between sobs. She stuck out her arm and pointed toward the bank. "She went that way, but she said I couldn't come."

"Ok sweetheart. I'm going to go find her, alright? Everything's going to be ok." Navarro shot to his feet and began running across the plaza toward the Woodman, as he spoke to Jacobs over his earpiece. "Did you hear that? She told the girl she was going away. Something's going down Jacobs! Call it in!"

Navarro tried to push his way past more people

on the sidewalk as he peered through the tall panes of glass to find Janice's figure walking into the foyer of the bank. He could see her drop her purse, as he shoved his way through the crowd. Something was happening because he could see a couple of the bankers begin to stand up from their desks and look in Janice's direction. As Navarro found a hole through the crowd and broke into a dead sprint for the tower doors, he saw Janice drop her long coat to reveal several pounds of C-4 strapped all over her body. Then it all went white.

****

Agent Jacobs had exited the car and was running after Navarro, a good fifty feet back when the deafening deep and full BOOM resonated from inside the bank, followed quickly by a blast wave that sent Jacob crashing to his knees; his view of Navarro obstructed by the explosion of fire and smoke. Jacobs felt the weight of the blast forcing him down into the pavement as he struggled to muster the strength to right himself.

The ringing in his head was mind numbingly painful and all-encompassing until it was eventually joined by the sounds of nearby screams as Jacobs regained his hearing in his left ear. Stumbling to his feet, he looked up to see the entire corner of the Woodman Tower missing all the way up to the 20th floor at least. Jacobs could hear the building groan, as it struggled not to buckle from the detonation. Navarro was nowhere to be found, but then again the plaza was covered in debris and bodies. Jacobs could see Tiffany, standing about exactly where she had been before, now bleeding from the face while some stranger tried to comfort her.

Jacobs looked down, fighting his double vision as he typed the numbers into his cellphone. He brought the phone to his right ear first but couldn't hear a thing, so he switched it to his left to find an operator asking for his SCID. He tried to speak but ended up choking as the dust around him immediately clung to the insides of his throat. After a violent string of coughs and hacking, Jacobs tried to recall his SCID number.

"Uh, yeah......uh I don't know. This is Jacobs, Agent Eric Jacobs. I need.... No! I don't know my SCID, dammit! I need help! Navarro, uh.... he's down." Jacobs struggled to speak consistently as he winced through the pain. Peering down, he only then noticed the pieces of rebar dug into his gut and thigh. "Ah crap. Um.... the woman, the mark, she .... she detonated something inside the building. There's dead people everywhere. You gotta....do... uh something."

Jacobs fell over on his side and dropped his

cellphone. Reaching out for it, Jacobs suddenly felt like the world was spinning around him and he couldn't help but sink to the pavement, trying to find some solid ground to support himself again. As his cheek rested against the ground, he looked off into the distance and watch the scurrying of people; everyone running around in panic. If they could all just slow down for a moment, just a moment, then perhaps everything would be fine. Jacobs clung to that thought, thinking it over and over again, until he grew tired and stopped.

****

ALBATROSS UNIT

Locke looked out across the floor of Agents; watching them desperately try to field in all the calls as the room had suddenly lit up with traffic only moments ago. Eugene was still in his office, now turning on every screen to a different news channel, waiting for some kind of official response. Locke looked down at his tablet, assessing the data that they currently had. All of his agents were either reporting an incident or were unresponsive. It seemed none of them had enough time to prevent an occurrence before it was too late. A message popped up stating that the White House was making a statement, and so Locke returned to his office and brought up the live feed just as the Press Secretary took the podium.

"Uh we've been flooded with information, and we're still trying to sort through it all, but it appears that at 12 p.m. central time, around 123 major cities across the continental U.S. suffered individual violent attacks of some kind or another. We've received reports of bombings of commerce buildings, mass transit stations, tourist locations, and worship centers. We don't have hard numbers yet, but the death toll is estimated to be in the tens of thousands.

"We've yet to hear of anyone taking responsibility, but we have our individual agencies following up on leads as we speak. The White House is currently asking the American people to stay in their homes or seek shelter, and not to assemble in any large masses until we can provide more information on these vicious attacks. Local authorities have been given the full support of the White House to take measures to enforce a strict curfew and clear the streets in highly populated metropolitan areas. Please do your best to cooperate and get home safely. Again, we have no accurate data to support any theories as to who orchestrated these attacks or why. I'll take a few brief questions."

The press room lit up with hands and call outs from several reporters as Locke turned to look at Eugene. Riley had attempted to extract something from Stoke before the compound was attacked. Perhaps they could have prevented some of this if she had only had a few more seconds alone with Stoke. Either way, the blood of the American people was currently running over the hands of the Albatross Unit. It was their marks that made these acts of destruction take place. Suddenly, the screen went fuzzy as static distortions rippled in and out of the broadcast until the screen went black and slowly refocused on a dark figure sitting on a stool in the shadows.

"Hello there, and good afternoon, America." The voice was masked in several layers of alteration to both hide the original tone and sex of the speaker. The lighting of the broadcast was also expertly placed to hide enough of the figure for one to determine the gender. "We imagine you are a bit lost for words at the moment, so we will provide the narrative. Today's attacks were a gesture to each of you, as the starting pistol signals horses to sprint, to recognize that this is the beginning of your end.

"We are the House of M.O.R.S., and we have come to put an end to this world." Locked sighed as he sunk down into the chair next to Eugene. It was never a good sign when a shadow organization felt comfortable enough to name themselves to the public. "Take a moment to let that sink in. There is nothing you can do. Yes, some of you will remain, but those chosen few have been preordained and there is no room left on the list. Things have been put in motion as of noon today that will soon end all the things that define your daily lives.

"We won't bother you with a countdown clock, as we do not encourage you to worry yourselves over the few days, hours, and minutes that you have left. Instead, you should do whatever it is you feel the need to do. Lock yourself away, or go out and gorge yourselves on every indulgence you can get your hands on. Either way, you will not survive the finality that awaits you. Your worth has been determined by better beings than you, and there is nothing that can be done at this point to change your fate.

"Do not let this despair cause you loneliness, America, for the rest of the world will know your pain and fear by the end of evening. Even now, brothers and sisters, mothers and fathers across the globe are making preparations to personally strike terror into the very veins of their fellow countrymen and women. This has been long in the making, and when the smoke clears tonight, there will be no doubt of the magnitude of our influence. Take heed in the knowledge that you are not without a doubt that your end is near. After today, there will be no more bombings executed in the name of the House of M.O.R.S. Those of you that have survived this introduction will meet a different kind of death soon enough."

"Finally, to our friends in the special operations collaborative known as the Albatross Unit, we have a special message." Eugene sat up and glanced back at Locke. "We have tolerated your meddling for long enough. Since we do not know who you are, save for a few key figures, and we do not currently know where you are, we will apply your punishment to the agencies you left behind. The loved ones of significant heads within the C.I.A., F.B.I., Homeland Security, N.S.A., D.E.A. and the Secret Service have been procured by our people. Should you choose to interfere with our plans anymore, these individuals will meet a grim fate."

The screen went dark and eventually returned to regular programming. Locke took a brief moment to take it all in before rising from his chair and turning off the screen. The expression on Eugene's face accurately portrayed the way Locke currently felt; uncertain and unhinged. Locke shifted his gaze out to the command center, where his agents were all watching the news on the giant screen, likely feeling the same as he currently did.

"Are we really that safe from discovery?" Eugene stood up and looked out at the command room with Locke.

"No, but that's not the point. If they had the time they could figure out who a majority of us are, but they are clearly focusing on their own timeline right now."

"Do you have family out there? Anything I can do?"

"Yes, I do, but they were moved to a safe place before I took on this position, as with most of the families of the people that work here. Either that, or they don't have a family to protect. Now it seems we need to have another thing to add to our list of time sensitive tasks."

"Right. Finding those people." Locke nodded and walked out to the balcony overlooking his staff.

"Listen up people. This is on us! We knew something was on the verge of occurring, but we failed to discover what that was before it was too late. Too much has slipped through our fingers. Today has been a day of days, but we cannot let it end like this. I have assumed that Panama was not the only cult campus for the Church of MORS. So we can expect those other members to be striking around the world over the next few hours. The agencies of the world can deal with those events that have yet to happen this evening, but we have our own tasks at hand. The people behind M.O.R.S. were not expecting us to the hit the Panama camp this morning, which means that there is likely something in the recovered data that we can use. So get your shit together and let's get to work. God knows the world is depending on us now."

8 WHAT'S IN A NAME?

LOS ANGELES, CALIFORNIA

Juliet stood there, wrapped within her thick satin curtains, looking out of her condo's window at the city below. A little past midnight, she had hoped the majority of people would have gone home to their families to support each other in whatever ways they could. Instead, the streets were filled with chaos. Everyone was rushing about, they couldn't go fast enough, trying to outrun their personal panic attacks. Looting, setting things on fire, screaming, the city was on the verge of a full-fledged riot, and she couldn't blame them. Their eyes had been opened to the evils of the world, and she almost felt sorry for them. They knew but only a small taste of fear and certainty that wickedness exists within the same space that they inhabited. She took a sip from her glass of wine as she heard the knock. Sighing, she left her view, grabbed a shirt and headed for the door.

"Good evening, Ms. Cubro." In hallway stood a well-dressed man in his fifties with an expression on his face that spoke of an even mix of exhaustion and annoyance.

"Technically its good morning, Director." Juliet stepped aside and allowed Director Locke to enter. Closing the door behind him, she walked to the kitchen. "Can I get you a drink?"

"Yes, please. Do you have something other than wine?" Locke took off his coat and hung it on a hook.

"Not a fan?"

"Not tonight." Juliet smiled and walked past her wine rack to the bar cabinet sitting off from the fridge. She fiddled through a few bottles before holding up one for Locke to see.

"How about some Soju?"

"You have Korean liquor? Wonderful. Is it from the States?" Locke stepped to the window and looked out over the city; a limousine at end of the block sat engulfed in flames.

"I think you know better than that. Real Soju

can't be sold in the States, Director, due to the fact that it's alcohol content is completely unregulated in Korea. Thus, I bought this bottle in Korea, just outside of Osan." Locke smiled and nodded, as Juliet grabbed a couple glasses. Juliet brought Locke a glass and then sat down at a table near the window. She waited for Locke to take the first sip and was pleased when he seemed to sigh in relief at the taste.

"Thank you. As much as I am impressed by your taste in Korean spirits, that's not what I came here to talk about." Locke joined her at the table, and took another sip. "I'm going to need your help with M.O.R.S."

"I already told you that I'd be willing to assist your agency's efforts."

"I'm afraid I need more than simply your assistance, Ms. Cubro. I need my men and women up to par with your capabilities. I need to understand what it is that you are, and how my people can get to that level." Juliet stared across the table at Locke, reading the seriousness in his eyes. Locke didn't know what he was asking for, so she would have to inform him.

"Follow me, Director." Juliet rose from her seat and took Locke down the hall, past her wardrobe, past the main bath, to the library. Walking up to the eastward shelf, she reached up and pulled on the spine of an old copy of Shakespeare's Romeo and Juliet. A latch released and the bookshelf shifted inward, revealing a passage way to another room. Juliet looked back at Locke and smiled. "Don't act like you're surprised by any of this. I know you bugged my apartment with mics and cameras and whatnot."

"You knew?" Locke followed her through the bookcase and down a short passageway that opened up to an armory room.

"I agreed to help you, and since I currently have nothing to hide, I felt generous enough to oblige your needs for security. Do you bug the residence of all your staff?" Juliet flipped a switch to reveal the room to be a lot deeper than it initially appeared, exposing a tall metal cylinder at the end of the room.

"Yes, to some degree or another. Consultants with access levels like yourself and Eugene require a bit more than others." Locke scanned the walls, impressed with Juliet's collection of firearms and other weaponry. Each rack held a different weapon, from a different country, designed for ultimate destruction.

"Ha. Well I hope you weren't keeping it a secret from Gene, because he's currently watching the feed of my cameras." Juliet looked up into the corner at the smallest of small dots on the wall and saluted. "Hello, Gene."

"He did not." Locke sighed. "You know you're the only person to call him that, and not get a look of a distain in response. Why is that?"

"It's something I used to call him before all of this, when he was innocent. I think he hates it when I call him that too, but I don't care."

"Either way, this awkward situation you've now placed me in is a perfect example of why I'm here. How can you tell who's currently watching the feed?"

"Nothing goes on in my home that I don't know about. After you installed your surveillance gear, I synced my implanted tech with your network and planted a reverse algorithm so that I could track who was watching and when. It was only fair, in my opinion."

"Fair enough, I suppose." Locke finished his drink and set it down on a table next to Juliet's bullet making setup. "Now how can I get that type of advantage in the hands of my people? I see you have your own personal teleportation chamber here. Teleportation alone would significantly increase my team's efficiency."

"I'm sorry, but it's not something that can be done, Director. It's not a matter of withholding technology, but a mere case of genetic makeup. Your people, no matter how capable, are simply not designed to do what I can do." Juliet looked up at the camera, still sensing Eugene's active access. "I think it's time I told you how I came to be."

****

SARAJEVO
13 YEARS AGO

It was a hard life, but a simple life. Having been born and raised in Sarajevo, Edin Cubro knew of no reason to leave it. He had had aspirations as a young man, sure, and had even learned English in anticipation to travel the world. When he left the care of his parents at a young age, however, he ended up moving into the apartment where he would remain for the rest of his life. Not one for education, it was ironic to all but him when he spent the next twenty years of his life as a janitor at the local University. It was a booming campus, known for its school of Mechanical Engineering, where Edin had been assigned. Edin never once read the writings on the blackboard, glanced at the study guides in the trash bin, or listened in on a lecture or one of the group conversations in the courtyard. He swept the floors, emptied the trash, and cleaned the toilets.

After twenty years of keeping his head down, twenty years of mornings spent massaging the kinks in his neck, and twenty years of minding his own business, he chose a day in 1996 to lift his head and glance at a pair of slick suited gentlemen chatting up some students in the hallway. It was not unheard of for headhunters to fish for new recruits within the walls of the University, but there was something different about these two. Instead of flashing their company logo, handing out hats or t-shirts, shouting their slogan for any and all to hear, these two were quiet, stern and vague. They couldn't say who they worked for, but it was something new to the area, and they were looking for a select few to fill some positions quickly and quietly.

Barely a year since the apparent end of the civil war in Bosnia and Herzegovina, Sarajevo was still digging itself out from the rubble. Then, without ceremony or jest, an unnamed party donated millions to the city to assist in faster, better repairs. An unusual amount of secrecy surrounded the transaction, but somewhere between the cranes and bulldozers, handshakes and wire transfers, this unknown entity became the shadow benefactor that helped Sarajevo back to its feet. In return, a patch of land was secured several miles east of the city, in an empty valley, with one road in and out and all the privacy that money could buy. A gate and guard post was erected overnight to secure the road on the edge of the city, and although Edin did not usually speculate on matters which did not concern him, he assumed the recruiters represented whatever had been built at the end of that now restricted road.

When Edin finished his tour of duty for the day, it was nothing short of a surprise when he found the two recruiters waiting for him outside the maintenance closet. In the most straightforward manner Edin had ever witnessed, the two offered him a position at what they called "the facility." He would hold practically the same duties as his current position, but his hours would be longer and his every move would be supervised. They promised him better pay and benefits than the University, so long as he would agree to their terms of confidentiality regarding whatever he happened to witness at "the facility." They shook his hand and told him to sleep on the offer, giving him a place and time to present himself if he accepted. Edin started his new position the next week.

For the next four years, Edin would board a bus at five in the morning and ride it for the hour journey along the road to the plant; watching the sun rise on the way there, and fall on the trip back. Even after officially accepting the position, Edin was never told who exactly he was working for. There was no logo on the building, no name on the letterhead, and no embroidered patch on his uniform. Edin had access to the majority of "the facility," as he was tasked to maintain a strict degree of cleanliness throughout his area. For those areas which he was not granted access, a night shift of janitorial staff was assigned. Like most of the local employees, Edin was placed in a lower tier of security clearance. With the exceptions of some of the big brains recruited from the University, most of the higher tiers were filled with preexisting personnel who were relocated from out of country to work and live on the grounds.

Edin knew to keep his head down, just as he knew that there was a long line of people that were waiting to replace him should he ever screw up. For that reason, he did as told, and tried to curb his curiosity to a level that wouldn't attract attention. With that said, security was so tight within the walls of "the facility," that Edin really had little to no idea what was actually going on. Of the few things he knew, he was certain that the work being conducted was meant to be kept secret from more than just the residents of Sarajevo, but the rest of the world as well. With the engineers and chemists, biologists and psychiatrists on staff, Edin could only assume the type of experiments that went on behind the many closed doors on site was related to human experiments.

Edin's suspicions were only substantiated by the severity of punishment applied to any breaches within the employee confidentiality policy. A violator would not only be removed from the roster, but erased all together. Whispers of midnight abductions were heard of now and then. Neighbors would deny the existence of someone who shared their building for years. Loved ones would be silent or be silenced. Names would never be mentioned again, and a new person would board the bus the next day.

Suspicious or not, Edin remained quiet and went about his daily duties. At the end of the day, Edin would remove his uniform, return all items to the maintenance supervisor, exit through the metal detectors and mandatory pat downs, and board the bus back to town. After four years of that same routine, Edin was content. It was on his ride home one December night, however, that Edin decided to look out his window. It was at that one moment that he glimpsed something moving behind the brush near the edge of the road. It wasn't an animal, but a small child searching for cover from the spread of the headlights. Edin didn't look twice, or make any mention of what he saw. He knew that to do so would damn both the child and himself and possibly everyone on the bus as well. Instead, he rode the bus into the city, walked home, ate his dinner and went to bed.

When he found himself tossing and turning in his sleep, unable to get rid of the thought of that small child, alone in the night, Edin rose up from his slumber. Dawning some dark clothes and a coat, Edin grabbed a flashlight and a pair of binoculars as he snuck out of his apartment building. Keeping to the back alleys, Edin made his way to the perimeter of the city, the outside street that passed by the secured land and the restricted road. Staying within the shadow of a tall building, Edin peered through his binoculars and scanned the area behind the security fence.

As the worker's bus never reach speeds north of 30 to 35 miles an hour, Edin figured there was somewhere between twenty to thirty miles of land between where he stood and the facility. Twenty to thirty miles of hills, brush, and dirt; no lights, no structures, and nothing to guide a person but the one restricted road. A child, presumably escaping the facility, would have to keep to the ground and move in both a sporadic and strategic manner to cross such a distance without being caught.

Edin had no plans of scaling the fence and pressing his luck on the other side, nor had he any plans of standing near the fence to peek in. His current spot in the shadows was about 3 blocks away from the guard post, and for all he knew, the street in its entirety could have been monitored. So instead, Edin clung close to the side of the building, hiding next to a trash can, blending with the dark, and watched the fence. An hour went by, and nothing. A second hour passed, but still nothing. By the third hour, Edin was fighting with the temptation of heading home. He questioned why he was even there, and what he would really do if something did happen. Before he could talk himself into retreat, he heard a rustling sound from across the street and watched as a small figure climbed over the fence and plopped down to the pavement on the other side.

Edin stood there, frozen, unsure of what to do. If he had heard the rustling of the fence, someone else might have. If he took a step out from the shadows, someone might see him, and if someone saw him, he might never see the light of day again. He peered down the street toward the guard tower and saw no apparent movement coming from that direction. Looking back at the figure, he found that the child had seen him and was now staring directly at him while standing still by the fence. Edin met her stare for a moment. Knowing now that his conscience would not allow him to leave her alone, he motioned for her to run to him. The child continued to stand still for a moment, took a glance up and down the street, and then quickly ran across and into the alleyway.

When the child stopped a few feet short, Edin crouched down and offered his coat. Wrapping the child up, Edin picked her up and ran back through the alleys to get to his building. Avoiding the light as much as possible, checking before every turn, every door, every hallway, Edin eventually made it back to his apartment. Setting the child down just inside, Edin quickly locked the door, and then went throughout the apartment and closed the blinds and curtains of all the windows. The last thing he needed was some peeping tom.

Once he felt the apartment was secured, Edin took a deep breath, turned on the light in the living room, dropped down to his knees and motioned for the child to come into the room. Standing in the dark of the hall, wrapped in Edin's big coat, the little girl took a moment before eventually walking over to him. She had long blonde hair and looked to be about ten years old or so. Beneath the coat, it appeared that she had only a white shirt and shorts on. Edin shivered at the thought of this child being out in the cold with nothing but these two items to cover her. She was covered in dirt, from her head to her bare feet, and she looked to be starving.

"Hello, little one. My name is Edin. What's your name?" The girl simply stared back at Edin and made no motion to answer. "That's ok, you don't have to answer. You look hungry. Would you like some food?"

The girl stared at him for another moment and then looked around the room, almost as if she was figuring out the best routes of escape. When she had finished canvasing the room, she returned her eyes to Edin and nodded.

"Good. I'll whip up some eggs and toast, and then we can get you cleaned up a bit." Edin rose to his feet and took off to the kitchen. The child didn't immediately follow him, and so Edin went about his way to make the food while checking in on the girl's explorations. She seemed to want to analyze everything single thing in his apartment by picking it up, looking at it in the light, and then gently setting it down exactly as it had been.

After the girl had inhaled the eggs and buttered toast, along with three chocolate chip cookies and a tall glass of milk, Edin had taken her to the tub for a bath. He found awe in how calm she was and yet how intrigued she was by everything around her. She didn't seem to know what a bath was, or what the suds and bubbles in the water were, or why Edin was holding a towel wide for her when it was over. She remained silent, and so Edin explained what he could in hopes that she would somehow understand.

At the end of the bath, Edin gave her one of his shirts, which hung down to her knees, and then brought her to the bedroom. After tucking her in, Edin sat on the side of the bed until she fell asleep. At times in Edin's life, he had wished for different circumstances. Circumstances that included finding a woman to love, and then raising children with her. That life had never come for Edin, and so he couldn't help but cherish this moment with the little ball of innocence lying passed out under the blanket.

Realizing he only had a couple hours before he would be due back at the bus stop, Edin took some spare blankets and a pillow to the couch in the living room and prepared a place for him to catch some much needed rest. As he put the dishes in the sink and gulped down one last glass of water, he heard a whimper coming from the bedroom. At first Edin stood still, figuring the child was simply having a bad dream, but then the whimpering increased to a steady cry and then a sharp scream. Running to the bedroom, Edin opened the door to see the child clutching her forearm in pain as it glowed red beneath her skin. She looked up at him with tears in her eyes, but before Edin could reach out to her, she was gone; disappeared from the bed and the room. As the sheets and blankets fell flat to the mattress, Edin stood motionless, wondering what could have happened to that poor girl and what mess he had involved himself in.

*****

Six months had passed since that night, and Edin had not seen the little girl again. Every evening, on the ride home from the facility, Edin fought the urge to stare out the bus windows and search for her. Every night, before bed, Edin peered out his apartment window, hoping to see the little child running down the street, but he never saw her. Edin couldn't help but let his paranoia get the best of him at work. He paid less attention to his work, and more attention to the people around him. He thought for some time that he was being watched, but weeks went by and nothing happened. Over time, Edin forced himself to accept that he would never see the girl again and that it was unhealthy for him to continuously wonder and worry about her. One night in the summer, the first evening that he actively chose not to look for her, however, he heard a knock at his door.

Edin opened the door to find a child standing

there, in a white shirt and shorts, who immediately seemed to recognize Edin even though she didn't look like the face Edin had memorized in his head. This child was older, by at least two years, and stood at least a foot taller if not more. The girl immediately hugged Edin in the door way and then helped him close the door behind him. In the light of the living room, sitting across from each other, Edin began to recognize her a bit more amidst his confusion about her obvious physical changes.

"It's me, Edin! It's me! The girl smiled at Edin as she wrapped herself in a blanket on the couch. "I promise! I'm sorry I couldn't visit you sooner."

"Oh, don't worry about that, now, child. I'm just so surprised to see you! You look so different! You've grown!" Edin tried to speak with confidence, not wanting to worry the child with his confusion. "Now that you're in the talking mood, would you mind telling me your name?"

"I don't have a name, silly!" The girl seemed to find the idea of a name preposterous as she laughed at the inquiry.

"No name? But you must be at least twelve years old by now. Why haven't you been given a name?" Edin quickly scanned the room, making sure his windows were properly closed and covered.

"I am twelve, well sort of, but I don't have a name, not yet."

"Ah, I see." Edin didn't understand, but figured he wasn't meant to. "Would you like some food?"

What Edin didn't know about the girl was probably best. It was probably best he didn't know that the twelve-year-old siting on his couch was actually only about 2 years old. The child wasn't given a name, because a name didn't matter yet at this stage in her production. Production was the keyword, as the child was being produced by the facility, not necessarily raised. Produced for a greater purpose than being a little girl, with a name.

From the moment of conception, the child was under constant supervision of scientists. Every chromosome, every molecule of her genetic makeup was designed. Once it reached a certain stage in the surrogate mother, the fetus was transferred to a synthetic womb to be monitored until birth. Once born, the child accelerated in growth exponentially at a rate of almost six years every twelve months. Daily treatments of hormones, testosterone, proteins, amino acids, and genetic supplements were given to the girl either through food or injections. Her bones and muscles went through constant tear and stretch conditioning to allow for the rapid growth, with implants of a technical nature inserted and removed as she grew.

Basic human skills and languages were taught to the child, both in person and through subliminal methods. Every hour of her day and night was programmed for optimal information intake. She had a photographic memory along with an ability to process information at speeds uncommon to the normal brain. All of her training and teaching were kept to basic things until something specific would be assigned to her. This would occur during her third year of development, and thus she found herself afraid of what was coming. So, she found an opportunity to escape, once again, and seek out her friend Edin.

"Do you still like eggs and toast?" Edin opened her refrigerator and fished out a few things.

"I've only had them when I was here last. My normal daily consumption consists of supplements and prescribed nutrients." Edin looked at her, again in confusion, as he held a carton of eggs in his hand and milk in the other.

"Eggs and toast it is then." As Edin cracked a few eggs into a hot skillet and worked them around in some butter he watched the young girl take a seat at the dining table. "So, what happened, the last time you were here?"

"I was called back. I had a device in my arm that teleports me back to the lab."

"It teleports you?" Edin had no idea what that meant. "It sounded like you were in pain. Are you alright?"

"I am now. It was extremely painful at the time, as it was only the second time that I was teleported." The child looked down at her forearm and rubbed it a bit. "I'm sorry if I scared you. I didn't mean to, I promise."

"You're fine, child. Don't you worry about it." Edin slid the scrambled eggs on top of some buttered toast and placed the plate in front of the girl with a full glass of milk.

After the child had finished her food, along with a small plate of sugar cookies, Edin could tell she was getting tired. Though he was afraid of repeating that nightmarish event from before, he tucked the child in bed sat along the edge until she fell asleep. He had more questions now than he did before, but he figured his time was short and didn't want to ruin the evening with an interrogation of a twelve-year-old. Instead, he sat in a chair by the window and watched her fall asleep. An hour or two past before he woke to a glowing light resonating from his bed. He stood up just in time to see the little girl smile back at him before she vanished, this time without a whimper. Once again, he was left alone, wondering if he would ever see her again.

****

The third and final time Edin saw the child was nearly an entire year later. Arriving home from the grocery store on a Saturday afternoon, Edin found a tall teenage girl sitting on the floor outside of his apartment. Hoping that no one had seen her, Edin quickly opened the door and let the girl inside. Within seconds of locking the door, Edin was engulfed in a hug from the girl and she clung tight to him.

The girl now appeared to be in her late teens, stood about five and a half feet tall, and now had shoulder length brown hair. After the girl finally released Edin from the hug, she grabbed his grocery bags and took them into the kitchen. Edin slowly took off his coat and watched as the young lady put away his groceries with a huge smile on her face.

"You've grown so much! I barely even recognized you!" The girl smiled and grabbed some cookies from the tin before joining Edin in the living room.

"It's so good to see you, Edin. I've missed you

so much!" She hugged Edin again and then gave him a cookie as she plopped down on the couch. "I'm sorry it's been so long. I tried so many times to come see you, but the security at the lab has increased and it took me awhile to figure out a means to escape unseen."

"Well I'm just glad you're alright. Every day, I wondered how you were, what you looked like, and how you were being treated. I didn't know if I'd ever seen you again." The girl sighed, stood up and walked around the room.

"I don't want to go back there. Things have changed so much since I saw you last. They've done so many horrible things." She crossed her arms and shivered at the thought. "They have told me what I'm meant to be, and soon they'll give me a name that suitable for the task. I don't want to go, but I haven't figured out a way to stop it from happening."

"Can you run? Is there a way to stop them from taking you back?" Edin still didn't understand the workings of the girl's disappearances, but he saw the pain in her eyes and wished he knew of a way to help her.

Pain was such an elementary word for what the girl had gone through in the past year. As her body developed into its final stage, the experiments became more and more intense. No longer did they bend her bones and tissue, no longer did they treat her something new and fragile. Instead they broke her, again and again, every inch of her, only to make her whole to break her again. The teleporter was their way of testing her limits.

Like a 3D printer of sorts, the teleporter would recreate a whole version of the girl whenever it signaled for her. The device inside her, which they removed, upgraded, and reinstalled almost weekly, would keep record of every miniscule detail of her being. Part of that record was based on daily data, while the other parts were programmed in after she had been strapped down, opened up, and dissected. When she was broken enough, bleeding enough, on the verge of death, they would activate the device. The device would send a signal to the teleporter, while simultaneously destroying the girl's current form down to the molecule. On her third birthday, the girl had been recreated 147 times.

Her skin was not her own. Her blood was not her own. One hundred and forty times over, by that point, she had been remade an artificial being, and one hundred and forty times over, she has suffered. The machine used special ingredients to put her together, but put her together better. Her skin was made of a cool texture, still containing pores to breathe, but ten times the durability of human skin, with an enhanced ability to regenerate. Her organs were made with a type of fiber-reinforced plastic. Her brainwaves were based on continuous recordings of her current state. 147 times she would burn alive and come back through the machine, and each time she felt less pain. At first, she counted it as a blessing, but it did not take long for her to miss it; her pain being the last thing that was hers.

"There's nowhere to go where they wouldn't find me. I don't know enough about my anatomy to stop them from finding me, but someday I will."

She hoped that someday would soon arrive, as she was quickly running out of time. Not only were the scientists putting her body through their final tests of durability, but they were now subjecting her to task specific training, as her purpose had been assigned. She was to be a slave, a toy for someone's pleasure; a plaything that someone could use for all the things they wouldn't dare do to a real human. Her magnificence, her existence, was to be assigned to the sole purpose of pleasuring a human's personal urges for the remainder of their life. She was to be a gift to them, for their loyalty to the company that ran the facility. Soon, her brain functions would be dulled, her personality would be programmed, and her ability to feel, to want, to need, to hope for something would be washed out. She would be mindless and submissive.

"I don't think I should come here anymore, Edin." She rose up from the couch, and began folding up the blanket. "My presence only puts you in danger, and I would never want anything to happen to you."

"Please, don't go. Your presence is the only highlight of my day, my year! I think about you every day and wonder if you're alright." Edin stood up and placed his hands on either of her arms. "I know the risks. I always want my home to be a shelter for you."

"But why? You don't even know me. I don't even have a name for you to call me. You have no obligation to me."

"Because you're a child who deserves to be cared for. I may not understand any of what you go through, or why you even exist, but who am I to care about those things? You were a child that needed someone to help, and I am thankful to have been there."

"I don't want to go back there, Edin. I want to live in the world, the real world, with people like you. They want me to be this fake thing, this artificial fantasy for someone, but all I want to be is a girl, a normal girl."

"We all have our setbacks, sweetheart. I wanted things in my youth, things I never achieved or received. But you aren't me. You were made to be different and someone told you that you can't be what you want. You aren't like the rest of us, and yet you keep running away to be more a part of this world. You're in love with what they have denied you, and no one can fault you for that." Edin stopped for a moment and turned to his bookcase. "I have an idea.

"There's a book I have, it's a copy of an old tale. There was a girl who was born into a family full of rules and restrictions. She was told who she could and could not associate herself with, who she could and could not love. She was supposed to follow in the footsteps of her father and mother, but she found herself attracted to the exact thing that they had forbidden. She fell in love with a boy, and the world he represented. She was willing to give her life to be a part of his world, and free herself from the confines of the life she was brought into." Edin found the book and brought it down from the shelf. "Her name was Juliet, and I think that should be your name."

"Juliet." Edin handed her a book, a play written by William Shakespeare, called Romeo and Juliet. "I haven't heard that name before, or at least I haven't heard anyone by that name at the facility. I love it."

"I'm glad, you do."

"But it's only half a name, isn't it. Don't people have two names, or even three names at times?" Edin nodded and smiled at her enthusiasm. "Do you have more than one name?"

"I do, yes. My full name is Edin Cubro." The girl looked down at the floor, biting her lip with a nervous look across her face. When she raised her head to face Edin, she had a tear running down her cheek.

"Would you grant me your last name?" Edin raised his eyebrows in surprise. The girl had an earnestness about her face. "As if…. as if I were your daughter, perhaps."

"Uh…" Edin could not help but lose his composure, as a tear floated up into his left eye and caused him to step back and wipe it away. He had known this girl for a total of three days, three partial days to be correct, and yet she had been a part of his every waking thought since the night he first saw her. He had dreamed of having a family, and having a child that would intrigue him as much as she did. He looked up at her, seeing the innocence in her eyes, seeing the worried expression on her face, as if she was concerned that she had offended him. Edin wiped his eyes again and smiled. "It would be my honor, Miss Juliet Cubro."

"Thank you!" Juliet hugged the old man tightly, tucking her face into his neck. This was truly the first gift she had ever received, and it was marvelous.

"Now I must ask you a favor, my dear."

"Anything!" Edin grabbed a case from the bookshelf and pulled out an old camera from it.

"May I take a picture of you? In case I never see you again, I want to be able to see your face when I send up my prayers for your safety." Juliet blushed and nodded. She took the book and hugged it tight as she sat down on the couch and smiled for the camera. After the flash, Edin put down the camera and wiped a tear from his eye. "That's for just in case. I do hope I see you again."

When Juliet left Edin's apartment that night, this time via the front door and not teleportation, she was not aware that that was the last time she would see him alive. Had she known, she would have hugged him harder, kissed his cheek, and offered to tuck him in as he had for her. Instead, she simply waved goodbye and told him she would see him later, the next time she could get free. She then walked the streets of the city, under the stars and the moon, until she felt the device within her activate, and she was called back.

****

A week or so later, during his shift at the facility, Edin was pulled into a room and questioned by a security guard named Hendricks. They asked him if he had witnessed anything peculiar on the grounds of the facility. They asked him whether or not he had spoken of the facility to anyone he knew. They asked him about his private life and what he did with his spare time. Edin knew why they were asking him these things, but he wasn't exactly sure if they knew of his involvement with Juliet or if they were fishing for something within the lower tiered staff. When Edin had answered all of their questions, however, he was cleared and sent back to work.

Edin finished his duties for the day and boarded the bus home. He didn't feel right about the whole thing, and wondered if he had really been cleared, or if his every move would now be under a microscope. He found himself enraged by their disrespect, by their assumptions, after all the time and work he had put into his job. He found himself ignoring protocol and staring out the window, searching the tall brush for any sign of Juliet. When he arrived home, there was no one sitting outside of his door. She had never revisited him this quickly before, but he suddenly yearned to see her, to know that she was okay.

While making his dinner he heard a knock at the door. It was a gentle knock, and it caused Edin's heart to jump a beat. He ran for the door, but upon opening it, he did not find Juliet waiting in the hallway. Instead, Edin was met with the same security guard that interrogated him earlier, Mr. Hendricks, along with two of his men. They forced Edin back into his apartment and sat him down on his couch as they ransacked the place. Eventually, they found something, a single long strand of Juliet's hair.

They didn't ask for Edin to explain. They didn't question him about Juliet's motives, how many times she had been there, or what she had told him. Instead they bagged the strand hair, took Edin's access badge, and proceeded to beat him to death. He didn't put up much of a fight; he was an old man, and did not have the strength of the longevity to go toe to toe with them. He only tried to think of Juliet while he still had breathes to breath. When Edin's body could no longer take the pummeling, and he laid motionless on the floor, trying to match his overwhelming pain with an equally overwhelming love within his heart, he used the last of his strength to smile. Mr. Hendricks stared down at him, bewildered at the sight, and then shot Edin twice in the chest. Edin's body was discarded in a dumpster, three blocks away, and wasn't found until the trash collector made the rounds. Nothing was ever reported to the police, no inquiries were ever made, no official funeral service ever took place.

****

LOS ANGELES, CALIFORNIA
PRESENT DAY

"This is the life that I knew, Director." Juliet looked up at the camera and stared into it for a moment. A moment went by, and then she sensed Eugene logout of the feed. "There is nothing about me that can be replicated for your men. Even I have my limitations."

"That's a story, for sure, and I'm sorry to hear it. Isn't there something that you can give me? That portable teleportation device that you used to rescue the team in Nebraska. Is that something we can use?"

"Technically that wasn't a teleporter. To teleport, one needs a unit like this to recreate the subject, as well as the coinciding device inside me that records the data." Juliet pulled down the folded-up metal disc that she had used in Nebraska. "This is technically more of a magnet than anything else. When you activated it, it honed in my signal and basically pulled me to it at speeds faster than the eye could see.

"Had it been a teleportation device, your men, Eugene and Agent Harper, would no longer be human, but merely replications of themselves." Juliet put the disk back on its shelf. She could see the desperation in Locke's eyes, but knew there was nothing she could grant him that wouldn't also mean sacrificing the humanity of his people. "I'm sorry, Director, but your people are not drones like the ones at M.O.R.S.'s disposal. But that doesn't necessarily make them weak. Now, I agreed to help you, and I'm willing to join or even lead an assault team if necessary. Just say the word."

"I appreciate your candor, Ms. Cubro." Locke stood up and shook Juliet's hand. "I had a team that I would like you to be a part of. Please stop by in the morning so we can talk next steps."

"Will do." Juliet walked Locke to the door and closed it behind him. Returning to her wine bottle, Juliet sat down in front of her computer and continued perusing through the data that the Albatross Unit had recently acquired. She took a sip and looked up at the closest camera. Eugene was no longer watching, but she wished he was. There was still more to the story that she needed to tell him.

Joshua D. Howell

9 CARE TO DANCE?

NEW YORK CITY

The ballroom was filled to the brim with the most powerful players on the east coast; politicians at the city, state, and executive level. There were heads of the private sectors, police chiefs, lawyers, and everything in between. The private event was an annual function for this group, and they never met in the same place twice. Many coveted an invitation to the event, but few new people would receive one each year. The purpose was to allow key people in key positions to speak freely, outside the eyes of the law or the press, and come to agreement over matters while indulging in their primal desires; legal or not.

"Good evening, ladies and gentleman, and welcome to the 23rd annual gathering of the Fox Club!" The room lit up in cheers as the presenter raised a glass and everyone followed suit. "Now I'd like to remind you that this is a full weekend event for a reason. Tonight, the first night, is meant for you to shake hands and the like, but it's not the night for business. You know what you're here for, and what deals you're hopeful to make, but that talk is to be reserved for tomorrow, leaving Sunday for anything official. Tonight is a night for fun!

"You all have had long enough to mingle and get the pleasantries out of the way, now it's time for the real night to start." The lights went out and suddenly the room was lit with black lights and other colorful strobes throughout. "There are no rules here, so don't hold back. To encourage this atmosphere, a few young men and women are walking around with masks. So please, take one, relax, and partake in the evening!"

The room ignited in a roar as the music began to play, the lights began to swirl, and several naked co-eds took to the dance floor carrying serving plates of different festive masks for the guests to take. The room became a mix of liquor and sweat within moments. In the dark, everything was game, and none of the guests declined to participate. The only people not participating in the developing mass orgy were the security guards stationed at the floor's elevator and throughout the area.

The sheer knowledge of this event was likely

enough to get someone through the door, as the secrecy involved was unmatched. As the clock struck late, a new batch of attendees entered the room. The man in the middle of the new blood walked down the stairs onto the dance floor and began wading through the discarded clothes, the screams and moaning, shrugging off hands that tried to drag him down to join.

"Cool mask, man! Care to dance with me?" A half-naked, likely underaged, girl cut the man off from her search. Waving her away, the man continued striding deeper into the congestion until he finally stopped. The man stared down at an overweight, semi-nude Senator sniffing a line of coke off the spine of a passed out waitress.

Even in the dark, the Senator felt the presence of someone standing over him. While he wasn't opposed to voyeurs in general, he felt something was off as the man was still fully dressed and didn't seem to be moving. He wiped his nose, slowly turned around and looked up to see a man in black suit, dawning an incredibly realistic and frightening full-head skull mask. The man with the skull then bent down and grabbed the Senator hard by the throat.

Bringing the Senator to his feet, the man in the mask released him and two more masked men grabbed him by each arm and began dragging him off the dance floor toward a private room. No one seemed to notice, as everyone else on the floor were knee deep in drugs and sex. The last thing the Senator saw before being thrown into a dark room was the pair of security guards lying on the ground in front of the elevator, unresponsive.

The man in the skull flipped on a light to reveal a circular room with a club style long lounge booth set up under a mirror that panned around the room. Hanging overhead was a disco ball and mini strobe lights. The Senator was thrown onto the booth along with his clothes. As the two men left the room, the Senator fumbled with his pants, trying to cover himself in front of the masked man.

"Having a good time?" The man in the skull mask stood there, arms hanging on the disco ball, leaning forward as he watched the Senator struggle with his zipper.

"What?" The Senator wasn't quite certain yet what this was. To his knowledge, he was in good standing with the Fox Club, but this could have been a shakedown of some kind. Whatever it was, the man in the skull mask, with skeleton hands, sent a chill down his spine.

"Are you having a good time, Senator

Richards?"

"I, uh, I was. Ha ha, until you showed up," Richards laughed nervously as he tried to find the man's eyes in the skull mask. Two black holes of darkness just stared back at him.

"Well I apologize for interrupting your little soiree, but I am in need of some information from you, Senator. Now, I understand you have plans this weekend with all your little foxy buddies, so I promise not to keep you too long."

"Fine. Fine. What do you want to know?"

"I want to know what the M.O.R.S. organization promised you." Suddenly, Senator Richards knew exactly what this was as he almost swallowed his own tongue upon hearing the name. As elite as the people of this club were, he could guess that maybe two or three other people in the building knew about M.O.R.S. and were sworn, just as he, never to tell. The man in the skull lunged forward and smashed his fist into the mirror near the Senator's head. "I believe I asked you a question, Senator! It would be in your best interest to answer me."

"In my best interest? Who the hell are you to tell me what may or may not be in my best interest? Do you know who the hell I am?" The Senator stood up, feeling the coke-induced confidence running through his veins. The man in the skull buried his fist deep into the Senator's gut an pushed him back down onto the booth to catch his breath.

"Oh no, you're right. I haven't introduced myself. You can call me Mr. Bones." The man took a bow and then slow turned his head back up to the Senator. Richards chuckled a bit under his coughing as he replenished his lungs with air.

"Oh you're a character, aren't you? What's with the getup? Is that supposed to scare me into submission?" Mr. Bones backed up a bit and looked down at himself.

"You don't like the suit?" The Senator chuckled again and then sat up as Mr. Bones leaned forward and pointed to his skull. "Oh you mean this. Well this is to remind you who's side I'm on."

"Side? What the hell are you talking about?"

"The side of the living, the side of human kind. The same human kind that your friends over at M.O.R.S. have promised to wipe out." Mr. Bones punched a mirror on his left and watched as the shards of glass fell to the booth. Shifting through the pieces, Mr. Bones picked one up that was almost 10 inches long. Turning back to the Senator, Mr. Bones gripped the shard of mirror in his glove as he pointed it toward Richards. "Now you're going to tell me what you know, or I'm going start removing pieces of your face."

"You're crazy man! If I tell you anything, they'll kill me! If I tell you nothing, you'll probably kill me! What's in it for me?" Mr. Bones sprung forward under his skull was within inches of Richards' face as he flipped the shard of glass back and forth in his hand.

"What's in it for you?" Mr. Bones rammed the shard of glass straight down into the Senator's thigh, deep enough to hit the bone, and held it there as Richards screamed out in pain. "You may live through the night if you give me something useful. If not, well that coke will wear off soon, and then I'll do more damage than you can imagine while keeping you sober and breathing."

"Alright! Alright, dammit, I'll tell you what I know." Mr. Bones bent his hand to the side and broke off the rest of the glass from the piece still lodged in the Senator's leg. The Senator screamed again as he looked down at the piece of mirror sticking out of him.

"Don't worry about that, Senator. It's better if

you leave it be for now. Instead, focus on telling me what I want to hear." The Senator looked up with tears streaming down his face as he caught his breath and tried to focus.

"I was approached by a woman. I thought she was a lobbyist or something, trying to get me to protect whatever company she ran, but that's not what she wanted. She told me that I had been selected, that I had found a golden ticket, and if I did what she wanted, I would survive whatever is coming."

"What's coming, Senator? Tell me!"

"I don't know."

"Who was the woman, and what was her company?"

"I don't know!" Mr. Bones lunged forward again, pressing his skull into the Senator's forehead. "I don't know! All they wanted was funding, and influence in the Senate. I was just as surprised by the shit show on the television as you were. You think I'm interested in a nuclear war or whatever crap their planning?

"I helped pass zoning laws for my state that would benefit M.O.R.S., as well as voting on certain trade bills and laws surrounding them in the Senate. Outside of the Senate, I would move money from certain government resources to be accessed by the woman and her pals. I never knew what they were using it for. All I knew is what she made very clear to me, that I would die, and that all those I knew and cared for would die too. I was doing it to protect them!"

"Don't sensationalize it, Senator. You were protecting yourself, and your interests, at the cost of innocent lives that you didn't need to know or care for. The lives that were lost are on you."

"Don't put that shit on me. I didn't know!"

"You didn't want to know! But you didn't need to be told the details to know what you were involved in." Mr. Bones stepped back and leaned against the wall while looking down at the Senator. "How will you be protected? What did you buy for you and yours?"

"I was given a number. If I have questions, I call it. Well you can bet your ass I called it after watching that broadcast." The Senator winced in pain as some blood spurted out of his leg.

"And?"

"And they told me to wait, to be patient. When the time was right, I would be retrieved. They didn't give me a date, a countdown, or any sense of what was coming. They only assured me that it was, in fact, coming and that I should be ready."

"Give me your phone, Senator." The Senator winced again as he reached down and dug the phone out of his pocket.

"The number is listed under 'M,' and it goes to an auto-assistant that sounds as generic as a dentist's office." Mr. Bones took the phone and put it in the breast pocket of his suit jacket.

"Thank you, Senator. You didn't give me much, but you gave me something." Richards nodded, clenching his bleeding leg as Mr. Bones turned toward the door.

"Yeah, yeah. Now get me to a freaking hospital, will ya?" Mr. Bones stopped and turned around.

"Oh no, Senator. You'd miss your party! Now I know our little chat has thrown a wrench in your mood, but you gotta get back out there! Here, Senator, let me help you get your groove back." Mr. Bones reached up and grabbed the disco ball. Yanking down from its chain, Mr. Bones stepped forward and smashed it down on the Senator's head.

While the shining ball rested on the Senator's shoulders, thick streams of blood began to pour down his neck. As Richards fell over to his side and stayed there, Mr. Bones dipped a boney finger into the blood and stepped up to the lounge mirror to write a message: "Mr. Bones was here, party on."

Joshua D. Howell

10 THAT SNOWDEN GUY WAS RIGHT?

ALBATROSS UNIT

"Somebody tell me who the hell this Mr. Bones guy is!" Locke slammed his fist down on the table as he addressed a room of his top agents, as well as Eugene and Juliet. "In the two weeks since the attack, this creep with a skull for a face has killed seven of our leads! I want answers!"

"All we know is that he's resourceful." Eugene leaned forward as he tried to be helpful for once. "He's been sighted with a team of highly trained professionals. Each person he hit had their own set of bodyguards, and that didn't seem to make a difference."

"He left notes with the bodies, threatening to do the same to anyone else connected to M.O.R.S." Locke pushed a button and displayed the a grid of photos. "These are the people that we've been tracking based on the data from Panama. The ones in red, obviously, are the ones Mr. Bones has disposed of."

"Is this necessarily a bad thing? Seems like the guy is cleaning the slate a bit, helping us out." said one of the Agents in the back.

"You want to keep your job, Agent Henry?" Agent Henry nodded immediately. "Then keep your dumbass ideas to yourself. This Mr. Bones character is reckless and quick to kill. I don't care who he is, he's costing us leads that we could have tapped."

"Then why haven't we? That's a hefty list of names up on that screen. Why don't we have them in the cellar, right now? They should be chained up until they talk!" Juliet looked at Eugene as he spoke, impressed that he was participating this much in the conversation.

"Why do you think, Eugene? Red tape, rules, higher ups calling the shots. Half of these people are untouchable. We can only play big brother on as many of them as we can and hope to find something." Locke switched the screen to show active pinpoints for all of the names they were tracking.

"Sounds like a load of crap to me, boss. We're just sitting here and waiting around for something to happen, meanwhile the doomsday clock has stopped ticking all together. On top of that, we still don't have a damn clue where the hell they took Riley." Eugene stood up and walked out of the room. The rest of the agents watched him leave and then returned their attentions to Locke.

"Gene!" Eugene didn't respond to Juliet's call, however, and proceeded out into the command center.

"Let him go. And yes, I've considered the possibility that he and/or any of you could be Mr. Bones. Had I not bugged your homes and kept eyes on you, I wouldn't be certain. Mr. Bones has access to similar or the same info as we do, and I need each of you to land some credible information before he wipes everyone off this list." Locke moved onto the next slide. A listing of all the factions of M.O.R.S. popped onto the screen:

M.O.R.S.

1. **The House of M.O.R.S.**
2. **The M.O.R.S. Initiative**
3. **The Hand of M.O.R.S.**
4. **The Church of MORS**

"From the data we collected in Panama, we have a firm grasp on the definitions of the different factions of M.O.R.S. The House of M.O.R.S. refers to the four heads, the four names that make up the acronym, as well as their administration. The M.O.R.S. Initiative refers to all of the scientific divisions planted across the globe, formerly managed by Samuel Stoke. The Hand of M.O.R.S. is comprised of the "ascended" individuals and any of the other foot soldiers loyal to the cause. The Church of MORS was a group of cult campuses around the world that preyed on the weak to either recruit for The Hand of M.O.R.S. or simply disrupt the local populations.

"It is a fair assumption that The Church of MORS has come to an end. Since the broadcast, there's no reason for them to be sneaky about this anymore. As in Panama, they recruited enough foot soldiers and disposed of the rest." Locke switched to the next slide which showed a world map. "While we were not able to find out names of the heads of M.O.R.S., we were able to find records of their history.

"In the late 1960's, a secret government group was formed under the codename: Echelon. This group operated under the authority of the United States, but was made up of a network of other countries that included the United Kingdom, New Zealand, Canada, and Australia. While there were other nations in the game, these were the biggest players. Together, with the United States, they were known as the Five Eyes.

"Now the declassified records will show that Echelon was created to spy on the Soviets and their communist allies in Germany, Hungary, Bulgaria, Yugoslavia, and a few others. With paranoia running rampant during the height of the Cold War, this would have easily been how the program was initially sold to the powers that be in order secure the private operations budget. By the end of the 20th century, however, Echelon was a completely different beast.

"Echelon had grown to become what the European Parliament would later describe as 'a global system for the interception of private and commercial communications.' There was chatter that Echelon was still in play long after the Cold War, and thus, investigations were opened, only to be closed again within a couple of years. Some of you may remember Echelon coming up again in 2015 as part of the Snowden leak. The reports claimed that the NSA was still using Echelon to spy on the world, and the media ran with it. As it turns out, those reports were nothing more than a scapegoat to hide the truth."

"Wait, so that Snowden guy was right?" an agent chimed in from the back.

"About a great many things, Agent. Now back to what I was saying before you so casually interrupted me. Echelon was the beginning stage of M.O.R.S. The founders of M.O.R.S. may not have been around when Echelon was first put in play during the Cold War, but they definitely took it over decades later and used Echelon to spy on the planet, overthrow certain governments, put key people into power, and plant footholds for their future operations. Echelon allowed them to operate completely invisible to the world, due to their uninhibited ability to listen in on every country's pillow talk.

"The deeper we dug, both in the data we pulled from Panama, as well as old casefiles from our own agencies, the more we found connections between Echelon and major economical and industrial events in the past sixty years. As far as we can tell, Echelon is still in play, though it is obviously under a different name. This is how M.O.R.S. was able to pick up on the safe house's video feed. This is how they are able to manipulate air traffic command to mask their flights. This is how they were able to secure so many V.I.P.S. into their employ; when you can see and hear everything, you know everyone's deepest darkest secrets.

"I've tasked our best people to seek out whatever version of Echelon currently exists, and then find a back door into it. If we can gain access to their network, we might be able to piggyback the signals to find where they're hiding." Locke changed the slide to another map of the United States with different glowing dots on it. "As of an hour ago, these are the locations that we were able to unencrypt from the Panama data. The Nebraska bunker is listed, so there is no discernable way to determine how current these facilities are without visiting them ourselves. I'm putting together teams for each of you to lead."

"Assault teams, sir?"

"Assault teams, rescue teams, kill teams, I don't

care what you call them. You'll be tasked to retrieve whatever data you can find. You will be responsible for assessing the worth of any personnel you find. If they are likely to be high enough on the totem pole to know something, you bring them in. If they are under duress or a hostage, you rescue them. If they are neither of these two things, you put them down." Juliet raised her hand, and Locke nodded toward her.

"I could have sworn you just gave us a lecture on how Mr. Bones has been putting down potential sources of information."

"Mr. Bones doesn't operate under our scope, and so I am not in any position to trust in his discretion. For all I know, he's killing these people merely for some half-hearted idea of avenging the human race, with no real care as to what information they may have possessed. Therefore, I cannot condone, or encourage his actions." Locke shut down the slideshow and turned the lights back on. "I do, however, have faith in the people sitting in this room. You've all been vetted, and thus you are cleared to make whatever calls you deem necessary.

"In an effort to streamline our unit's effectiveness, on-site interrogations are a must. You are all cleared for level 4 tactics, and I will require one supervising agent to provide a live link back here to base. We may be a black-ops unit, but we need to document our efforts. Any information as to the heads of M.O.R.S., their base of operations, or to the location of Agent Riley Harper, is to be immediately forwarded onto me." Locke tossed each seated person a folder. "In each folder, you'll find your assigned agents, your weapon and tech clearances, travel authorizations, and your assigned locations to investigate. I want my teams in the air headed toward their first location within 4 hours. Dismissed."

The group stood up and rushed out of the conference room, eager to assemble their teams and get to work. Juliet remained seated as she scanned her packet. Her network link to the database for all M.O.R.S. facilities was cut off after the raid in Nebraska. Still, upon entering any of these facilities, she should be able to link up to their resident networks and discover all the local information on their servers. Locke leaned against the table and looked down at her.

"Rest assured I put the most likely locations on your list."

"And how did you discern those, Director?"

"Calculated guesses to include previously known blueprints, tactically strategic positioning, and a few other factors that could presumably equal a higher chance of the location being a base of operations versus a storage locker." Juliet stood up and stepped toward Locke.

"Does Gene have a group?" Locke sighed and stared out the glass, finding Eugene in the command center, staring over the shoulder of an agent at a computer screen. Locke shook his head and looked back at Juliet.

"He doesn't, and I think you know why he doesn't. I won't lie, Ms. Cubro, Eugene is still too unpredictable for me. Not to mention, he's technically still just a consultant."

"So am I, Director."

"I know, but I'd rather keep him here, and keep him busy." Locke headed for the door.

"Don't you trust him, Director? You said it yourself, he's not Mr. Bones." Locke stopped and turned back to Juliet.

"He may not be, but he's just as dangerous. He still has connections at Reynold Pharmaceuticals. Since his extraction from Summerhill, Eugene has not held back from accessing his fortune and enjoying the finer things."

"I enjoy the finer things. You've seen my place." Juliet stood and walked towards the glass, staring down at Eugene.

"He used to be ashamed of it. After he was acquitted, he went off the grid. He didn't seek a luxurious lifestyle. When he grew tired of that, he didn't rent out a penthouse, he admitted himself into a psyche ward. He doesn't seem as reserved now as he was before we broke him out, and that concerns me." Juliet looked down at the floor and then back at Locke. "I know what you're thinking, but I don't intentionally prefer my allies in a docile state. Still, I've also learned not to underestimate someone's potential to misbehave."

"Just remember, Director, church boys often rebel at the first whiff of freedom from their over-protective parents. You wanna keep Eugene in the fold, don't give him a reason to leave it." Juliet walked past Locke and out the door, leaving the Director to lean against the glass and continue to watch Eugene from afar.

Joshua D. Howell

11 DON'T TOUCH MY FOOD

SOMEWHERE

The room was dark and damp. The air felt filtered, which supported the assumption that the place could very well have been located underground. The immediate space allowed for zero outside sound or light, and thus zero opportunity to adjust vision in the slightest in order to get a sense of the room's dimensions, exits, vulnerabilities, potential weapons, or anything else for that matter. This room was meant for one purpose, to detain and incapacitate its occupant. Trapped in dark, hearing nothing but one's own heartbeat, unable to move or see; it was a form of torture with a high success rate if used properly. For a weaker mind, the total and utter isolation could drive a person insane. Riley Harper, however, was not weak.

She had no idea where she was or how long she had been there. She remembered the crash in Panama, and being abducted thereafter, but that was it. When she awoke, she awoke in the dark. After feeling around, with her limited movement due to the straps, she discovered an IV drip plugged into a vein on her right arm, a catheter, and wristband of some kind that she assumed was to measure her heart rate.

She had no way of telling how long she had been unconscious. With the constant darkness and zero interaction with anyone, she also had no way of knowing how long she had been awake. She was not fed solid food or liquids, as she assumed the IV was suppling the basic nutrients to keep her alive. For lack of better things to do, she would frequently fall asleep, only to wake up feeling somewhat clean, as if someone had entered the room to take care of any mess.

In her early days with the F.B.I., Riley had made it a personal mission to volunteer for any and all torture sessions. From the moment she had signed up to become an agent, she was never short of people telling her how the odds were against her. She would never compare herself to a full-fledged Navy Seal or Marine Special Forces, but she enjoyed the chance to prove her superiors wrong by enduring whatever physical and psychological torture tests they could throw her way.

Once she had passed all the entry level, basic crap, she had made it a point to find the most intense trials. She would usually opt to participate in one of these between assignments, to keep up her game as she would say. These higher level, less advertised sessions would include everything from being abducted off the street to being released deep in the wild. Sometimes, Riley would be assaulted to the point of injury in the beginning, so that she would not be at full strength for the test. Injury of any kind can, overtime, severely affect one's ability to withstand obstacles that normally could be achieved while in a healthy state. Motor functions deteriorate, like an engine without oil. Brain functions tend to fluctuate while the mind is at constant odds with itself as it fights to process pain while simultaneous maintaining a clear enough head for decision making instances.

Though Riley could tell she had been fixed up to some degree after the accident, her dormant state, as well as the reliance on her IV for substance, was severely affecting her ability to remain alert. She fought to keep herself awake and ready for anything, but the silence and darkness engulfed her, and impeded her ability to remain vigil and lucid. Still, she was not weak. Like a predator, minimalizing everything down to its heartbeat to fool its prey, Riley conserved whatever energy she could as she awaited the opportunity to use it.

****

To keep her mind from dissolving into mush, Riley focused on the same thing, the one thing that kept her focus all those months in Panama. His name was Peter and he very well could have been the one for her. From the first day that they had met, he stood out. He was a P1, straight out of the academy, and he sure as hell showed it. He was eager for the day, vigilant on patrol, caring to those around him, compassionate to the less fortunate, and vindictive to those that preyed upon those less fortunate.

Riley picked him based on the qualities she had looked for in young men on other assignments; looks, willingness, and smarts. He didn't need to be a rocket scientist, but needed to be smart enough to keep his mouth shut. Most of the other men treated her like a foreign goddess who had come to bless their shores for the time being. They pampered her, tripped over themselves for her, and fought for her attention. Peter did not.

Peter obviously enjoyed their time together, and knew the potential career benefits of their arrangement, but he didn't seem to let it change him.

He didn't buy a suit from the corner store so he could take her to some five star restaurant that cost half his paycheck. He took her to his favorite fish and chips place, and then a disheveled old theater for a late night showing of a cult classic. He didn't shy away from inviting her over for fear that she would disapprove of his living conditions. He brought her back to his place after the second date, where they made out on his unmade bed. When she gave him a key to her apartment, he didn't overanalyze the situation to turn it into something bigger than it was. He just took the key, smiled, and then showed up that night to join her.

Perhaps it was the stress of the Seattle case that made her vulnerable. Perhaps it was the stark difference between Peter and the other men she had known. Perhaps it was his boyish charm and confidence. Perhaps it was something inside her that was finally ready to admit that she needed someone. Whatever it was, Riley had found herself waking up five minutes early just to look over at him. She began to hold his hand on random occasions. She'd plant kisses on his shoulder in the shower after a run. She would blush in a way she hadn't blushed since the homecoming dance of her freshman year in high school. Once she had allowed these small transgressions to occur, things that went against her normal strong and stubborn character, the rest of her caved in. Within the short time that she had resided in Seattle, she had fallen in love with Peter. Was it a reckless love? She was certain it was, but it was refreshing in a way that couldn't be denied.

Every night in Panama, as Riley fought to fall asleep in the heat, she had thought of Peter. She thought of the texture of his lips, the hair on his arms, the devilish curve of his smile, the blue of his eyes and, finally, the despair on his face when he had begged her to kill him. He was a beautiful creature that was taken from her, tortured, and then sent back to her just in time to die. She was not given time to say goodbye, or to mourn, or to hold his hand one last time. Every second she had waited, he grew closer to becoming a ravaging beast hellbent on killing everyone within the vicinity.

She could have commanded any one of the several surrounding guards to take the shot to end Peter's life. She could have turned away, so that the version of Peter in her mind remained a happy and content police officer. Instead, she took the responsibility on herself. No one should ever have to kill the one they love; to be forced into the position of choosing between ending their lover's life or allowing their lover to live on in agony. She had failed to save her love from the hands of M.O.R.S., and the act of killing him was both a mercy for Peter and a punishment for Riley.

So in her times alone, in the quiet, in the dark, she thought of him. She thought of where she could have been, had none of this happened. Would she have moved on after solving the case? Would she have finally taken a vacation and stayed in Seattle a while longer with Peter? Would she have woken him in the night, sat across from him in the bed, and confessed her love for him while streaks of city lights crept through the blinds to run and dance over their bodies? Would she have asked him to come with her? She never got the chance to find out.

When she was cold, she thought of the warm place she had found when wrapped within his arms. When she was frustrated, she thought of his smile and the tiny things he did to brighten her day. When she was scared... when she was scared, she thought of his bravery, his consistency, his willingness to run into danger instead of waiting for proper backup to arrive. If she could only have kissed him one last time. If she could only have told him the truth she hid inside her. If she could only have confessed that he was the one person to break down her walls and convince her to trust someone again. Though these thoughts of Peter usually ended with a tear or two escaping down Riley's cheek, they reminded her that she had genuinely felt for someone at least once in her life. That, in and of itself, was reason enough for Riley.

****

When Riley woke the next time, once again finding herself alone in the dark, she noticed something different. The IV needle had not been taped down to her skin and was slowly sliding out of her vein, and out of her arm altogether. Someone must have adjusted it during her sleep, and forgot to secure it properly. Riley flexed and twisted her arm in order to the help the needle find its way out of her. Once it plopped out of her, Riley balanced the needle on her forearm, allowing it to continue to drip onto her skin. Tilting her arm a bit, Riley patiently waited for the liquid to puddle and then form a stream that led down to her wrist. Unlike handcuffs, the straps over her wrists were tighter and a bit more hefty to the point that simply breaking her thumb would not be enough to slide out of the restraints. Adding moisture, however, could sway the odds a bit.

Riley waited patiently as enough of the IV leaked down her arm to pool between her wrist and the straps. When the needle finally rolled off her forearm, Riley knew her time was limited to make this work. She tucked her thumb into her fist and began to twist her wrist back and forth under the strap. She pulled up on her wrist, attempting to squeeze the muscles of her hand deeper into the straps. She was losing the moisture as each attempt failed. Finally, she slid her hand back enough to work her thumb under the strap and then little by little wiggle it out the other side to pull the rest of her hand through. She was out.

Her reach was limited to the shoulder straps, but she had enough to unstrap her other wrist, then the shoulder straps, the belt around her waist, and the straps on her legs and ankles. Before long, she was climbing out of the vertical bed and found herself kneeling down on what felt like a rock floor. As she gathered her strength, she felt around the walls trying to find anything useful. She was definitely underground in a cave like setting of some kind. She thought she found an outline for a door, but there were no hinges, no handle or knob, and nothing she could grab hold of or pull. She pressed her cheek against the door and tried to listen for something on the other side, but heard nothing, so she continued feeling around the room. Unless she was mistaken, the room was no bigger than a walk-in closet. The ceiling was eight feet high or so, and everything but the door felt like a natural rock surface. Perhaps this was an underdeveloped bunker, or perhaps they simply didn't feel the need to finish all the walls when the rock was enough.

Riley grabbed the hanging needle and broke it off from the IV drip. She returned to the door and ran the needle into the crack. She slowly slid the needle around the frame of the door, feeling for something for it to catch on. She found a deadbolt, but the space was too tight for her to slip the needle in and force the bolt out. She tried to etch away at the rock surrounding the bolt, but ended up breaking the needle. As Riley heard the pieces of the needle fall to the floor, she clenched her fists in rage and smashed them against the door again and again and again.

It wasn't long before she wore herself out and found herself slouched down to the floor, leaning against the door. She pressed her ear against the door once more and waited. Eventually, someone would come through that door to check on her. She could only hope that she had enough strength to make it count.

She had no idea how much time went by, and whether or not she had fallen asleep, but she was certain she was awake now as she heard the faintest of footsteps approaching the door. She felt around the floor until she found the broken needle. It wasn't much, but it would have to do. She heard a key slide into the door to unlock it, and then the door began to move outward from the room. Riley used all her might to spring up and grab whoever had opened the door.

Now, in an empty hallway with bright lights, Riley struggled to focus her vision as she forced the person against a wall with her hand covering the person's mouth. As her eyes adjusted, she found that she was holding a female nurse in green scrubs against the rock wall of a long hallway. The floors were tiled, and electricity was obviously flowing through the structure, but the rest was still rock. Perhaps this place was located deep inside a mountain somewhere.

The nurse had a surprised look on her face as she struggled under Riley's grip. Riley looked down to see the nurse's badge which only displayed her face, a barcode, and an insignia that spelled out M.O.R.S. Riley looked back up at the nurse in fury, pulled her off the wall and then slammed her head back against it, knocking the nurse unconscious. As the nurse collapsed to the floor, Riley quickly knelt down and began to strip her. Riley placed her wristband on the woman's wrist and then hauled her into the dark room and slammed the door shut.

The clothes weren't the perfect fit, but Riley made them work as she laced the shoes tight and began to make her way down the long hallway. Every couple feet or so was a door. Some of them had windows and descriptions while others, like the door for her cell, were blank and solid. Clinging to the walls to support her weight, Riley passed empty labs, classrooms, and storage closets. Finally, she found what appeared to be a breakroom. After verifying the room was empty, Riley snuck in and almost collapsed when she saw a sink.

Riley turned on the faucet and immediately shoved her face underneath to swallow as much water as she could catch in her mouth. She didn't realize how thirsty she had been until the water hit her tongue. Knowing that too much water at this point could make her sick, Riley forced herself up from the sink and made her way to the refrigerator. She opened it up to find several tupperware containers, each marked with someone's name, as well as random condiments and beverages. The normalcy of it all caught Riley off guard. Was she being held prisoner by a normal office full of Joes? She grabbed a couple containers and threw them to the ground until she found what looked like a peanut butter and jelly sandwich. She opened it up and inhaled the sandwich as she stepped back and surveyed the rest of the room.

The walls were lined with tall footlockers, each marked with someone's name. Riley looked down at the container in her hand, which had a label that read, "Tim." Scanning the lockers, Riley found the one marked "Timothy Hanes" and opened it. A set of clothes hung from a hanger, an old Walkman and a pair of sneakers sat on the top shelf, and a stack of comics sat on the floor of the footlocker; nothing she could use. Riley moved down the line of lockers to find a couple ones in a row that were locked. The name tags each had a rank next to the name.

Riley picked up a metal chair and slammed it down against the first locker, breaking off the lock. She opened it and found nothing of value. Picking up the chair again, Riley slammed it down against the second locker, breaking the lock. After opening it, she sighed as she only found more of the same. Riley picked up the chair once more, now beginning to feel the weight of it as she slammed it down against the third lock. Missing the lock, Riley fell forward against the lockers and groaned as she hit them hard. She took a deep breath and raised the chair again. Swinging it down hard against the locker, Riley broke the lock as she reached out to brace herself from falling over in exhaustion.

She opened the locker to once again find a set of civilian clothes as well as a couple personal items that were of no use to her. She was about to collapse down onto a chair before she saw something wrapped in a cloth in the back of the top shelf. She reached for it and immediately recognized the weight. Apparently, the guard that owned this locker wasn't one hundred percent confident in his job security, as he had snuck in and stashed a .45 caliber Beretta handgun into his locker. Riley ejected the magazine to find it partially loaded with 8 rounds, including one in the chamber.

Riley quickly loaded the magazine and shut the locker as she heard someone coming down the hall. She shoved herself inside one of the other lockers and shut herself in as a guard and another man in a lab coat entered the room and went to the refrigerator. The guard grabbed a can of soda and a container, which he threw into the microwave, as the man in the coat fumbled around in the refrigerator.

"What the hell? Who took my PB and J?" The guard began to laugh as the man in coat continued to dig around in the refrigerator. Riley took the opportunity and jumped out of the locker.

"Turn around and put your hands up." The guard barely flinched at first, but then saw that Riley was holding a gun and became compliant. The man in the lab coat slowly turned around and faced Riley with a frown on his face.

"How did you get out of your room, Agent Harper?" The man, which Riley could only assume was Dr. Hanes, looked more annoyed than frightened. Riley stepped forward and motioned for Hanes to take a seat as she grabbed the guard and pulled him over to a table. Sitting him down, Riley clocked the guard in the back of the head with the butt of her gun, knocking him unconscious. "Now why did you do that? You're only making things harder on yourself."

"Where am I? Tell me!" Riley kept the gun pointed at Hanes as she searched the guard's pockets. She grabbed his firearm, a set of keys, and an electronic keycard putting them in her pockets.

"Does it matter? You're not leaving." Riley grabbed the guard's handcuffs and threw them at Hanes. "Now what do you expect me to do with these?"

"Cuff yourself to that pipe hanging by the wall. Do it now, or I'll shoot."

"Oh no you won't. The sound will echo enough to give away your location." Riley stepped forward and cocked the gun. "Fine, fine!"

The man stood up on his tip toes to bring his arms high enough to get the cuffs around the pipe. He latched the final cuff around his wrist and then looked back and smirked at Riley. Riley fumbled through the man's pockets, nabbing his keycard. So far, no one seemed to be carrying a cell phone, likely because there was no signal this deep underground. Just as Riley was about to step away from Hanes, she noticed something blinking just beneath the cuff of his lab coat. Pulling up his sleeve she found a wristband with a blinking red button.

"Dammit!"

"Oh yeah, sorry about that. I pressed it while you were pick pocketing the guard over there. Next time, don't touch my food, bitch." Riley rammed her elbow across the man's jaw and then ran for the door as his head hung over, unconscious. Before Riley could open the door, however, it was kicked in and hit her square in the face. She fell backward and down to the floor, failing to rectify herself as the room was swarmed with guards dressed in black. With her .45 lying on the floor out of reach, Riley reached for the second handgun in her waistband, but was quickly kicked in the face by one guard as two others grabbed her arms.

They held her down and disarmed her before putting a thick strip of duct tape over her mouth and a blindfold over her eyes. Pulling her up, they began hauling her down the hallway as she struggled to get free. She was in the dark again, unable to see, but at least she could hear and she could tell they were taking her somewhere other than the closet she had been kept it before. She stopped struggling and once again conserved her strength; waiting for the next opportunity to strike.

Joshua D. Howell

12 KILLING AT THE PLAYGROUND

UTAH

"Agent Cubro, can you hear me? This is Captain Dorton, your pilot." Juliet opened up her eyes at the sound of the pilot's voice coming over her headphones.

"It's Ms. Cubro. I'm not an agent."

"My apologizes, Ms. Cubro. I have a status update for you." Juliet adjusted her headset as she came up from her nap. She looked across the cargo space of the V-22 Osprey and her assigned twenty agents. The majority of them were asleep, as it had been a long 48 hours.

Her team had raided three locations so far; each had been cleared out and booby-trapped. After clearing the traps, her team had meticulously searched each location to verify that nothing of value was left behind. So far, they had come up with nothing. The task was tedious and time consuming, which is why Juliet was glad that they had an Osprey as their transport. The United States government might have hated the production of this tiltrotor aircraft, but it was a favorite among special-ops teams. With one three-bladed proprotor on the tip of each wing, the Osprey is able to vertically land and take off from practically any open space. This meant that the Osprey didn't need a landing strip to land or take off from. Once in the air, the proprotors rotate to a 90 degree angle in less than 15 seconds to allow the Osprey to function as a turboprop aircraft capable of reaching speeds over 300 miles per hour.

"Go ahead, Captain."

"We are five minutes out from Hill Air Force Base. Looks like the entrance to your next facility is about halfway up the Wasatch Mountain range. With the heavy forestation around that area, I can't get this bird too far up. Director Locke called ahead and wanted your team to have some fresher weaponry than whatever you've been hauling around the last two days. There's a tactical convoy waiting on the tarmac for you." Juliet thought their current gear was sufficient, but she wasn't about deny new toys if they were being offered. Perhaps Locke had found new info that would support a greater chance of finding something at this location. "They've constructed a temp shelter for you and your team to gear up, and I've been informed that a portable armory has been set up for you to utilize as well. Once your convoy is on the road, I'll scout out a spot to land closer to the mountain range in case you need aerial support. Sit tight. We've already begun our decent."

Juliet sat up straight and turned on her tablet to go over the notes she had on this upcoming location in Utah. As with the previous three locations, the data only gave a basic ground floor layout of the facility and where the main entrance and exits were. She assumed these were available only because the majority of M.O.R.S. locations were previously owned and thus had some public record out there. Each location they had raided had undergone construction to allow for multiple additional floors and structures not on any public record. Juliet assumed the same for Utah.

She flipped a switch on her headset that allowed her to have a private conversation with her second in command, Agent David Yoke. Yoke was originally in command of this team, and had served as their team lead for several missions in the past, both before and since Albatross Unit came to be. Juliet had no intention of breaking up the band, or trying to rewrite the script with this team. She was capable of handling herself. She spoke with Yoke before missions and he let her run his crew.

"Yoke, you catch that?" Yoke nodded as he sat across from her in the cargo hold of the Osprey. As a common courtesy, Juliet had all conversations with the pilot relayed to Yoke's headset as well. "Anything you want to cover before we arrive?"

"Same as the previous three. We'll be on the lookout for any booby-traps. Game plan is to secure all sectors before we try to retrieve anything. The front man will have a live feed that links back to base. We'll take it slow and get it done."

"You get any sleep?" Juliet stretched her arms as she slouched back against the wall of the cargo hold.

"Enough to be effective. You? Do you sleep?"

"I do, and I did. Enough at least." Juliet smiled. "You do a lot of this type of stuff before Albatross?"

"Sure. Most of this crew was a part of my team under the Joint Special Operations Command. Before then, I was an undercover agent for the D.E.A." Juliet leaned forward.

"I bet that was interesting." Yoke nodded again.

"Interesting is a word you could use."

"Any long hauls?"

"Most of them amounted to a month or so, but there was one that lasted about three years. I was in deep with a KKK clan out of Georgia who wanted to step up their game a bit. Went from white robe meetings in the woods to hoarding explosives, among other things." Juliet could see the discomfort in Yoke's face as he talked about it. "It didn't end well."

After landing, the crew took a brief moment to look over the new equipment before loading up in the six truck convoy and heading up the mountain. Their notes indicated three breach points, and so at about a mile out, the trucks split into three groups. Juliet's truck continued up the dirt path while the others went off road between the trees. The whole thing felt a bit like deja-vu for Juliet, as she remembered what went down in Nebraska, but this was no time for hesitations. The truck came to halt in front of a massive blast door, as Juliet and Yoke hopped out with their four other agents, two began setting the charges.

"Team one is in position."

"Team two in position."

"Team three in position."

"Breach!"

The charges opened up a hole large enough for Juliet and her team to enter the facility, which they found to be pitch black. Once inside, the team flipped to night vision as they quickly made their way down a hall. It didn't matter if the facility appeared to be abandoned, the team had to cover it inch by inch before they could be sure it was secure. The hallway led to a receiving area with chairs, a check-in desk, and monitors on the walls. Motivational posters were framed on the open wall space, and pamphlets about the House of M.O.R.S. were neatly displayed in racks along with other reading materials.

"What is this, a M.O.R.S. orientation facility?" Yoke looked back at Juliet.

"Could be, who knows? Keep your men on high alert." Juliet looked up at the ceiling to a black round camera suddenly move and flash red. "Shit, we're being monitored. Get ready!"

The team divided and found cover as they each trained their weapons on one of the two doors that led to the reception area. Juliet kept her eyes on the camera as it seemed to focus down on her while the red light blinked. Suddenly, one of the television monitors on the wall came on, and Juliet saw a familiar face.

"Hello there! It's good to see you again." A young woman in a business suit appeared on the screen, standing in front of a M.O.R.S. insignia. "Thank you for visiting our facility. As you can see, the House of M.O.R.S. is on the verge of doing great things in this world, and we are thrilled to see that you've come to be a part of it. Why don't you follow me as I give you a tour of our campus here in the mountains!"

"Stand down, it's just an automated tour. Teams 2 and 3, sound off." Yoke signaled for his team to converge on the door to the left as it automatically opened, the lights above slowly starting to flicker on. Juliet brought up the rear of the group as she gave one last look down the hallway they first came from. She had a feeling, and it wasn't a good one.

"Team 2 is good. We've encountered an automated assistant giving us what looks to be a tour of the facility."

"Team 3 here. We've got the same."

"Stay vigilant. Yoke out." Team 1 progressed down a hallway, following glowing arrows that lit up the computer screens leading them into an area full of mannequins showing different stages of anatomy; muscles, bones, organs, tissue. Another screen lit up and the young woman once again addressed the group.

"The House of M.O.R.S. recognizes your hesitations about the master plan, but we assure you that in good time you will understand everything. The human race, though massive in quantity, remains ultimately fragile. Digesting the wrong foods, breathing in the wrong air, drinking the wrong liquids can cause anything from a mild cold to a complete physical shutdown of the body. The M.O.R.S. Initiative, our science-fueled branch, is here to help the human race move forward into better, stronger beings."

More arrows led the team down another corridor as the assistant spoke about how donating time and money to M.O.R.S. was not only ensuring one's personal future, but a better future for generations to come. Juliet kept looking behind as the arrows led the team where to go next. Each room or corridor had glassed in rooms with mannequins dressed in clothes, posed as if they were workers at the facility, or as if they were acting out whatever setting the room was designed to look like. One room resembled a park, and a mannequin family appeared to be having a picnic. Another room resembled a busy stock exchange center, and mannequins were at each other's throats with their arms raised with clenching fists. The tour guide kept spewing vague nonsense after nonsense as the tour continued.

"Yoke. Something's not right. We're being pushed deeper into the compound. This feels like a trap." Juliet kept her rifle trained on the open corridor behind them as the team progressed from exhibit to exhibit. She looked over at Yoke and saw him nod in agreement as he kept his weapon trained ahead.

The next corridor led to an intersection with two other corridors, as all the walls were essentially more display cases. These ones showed laboratories, operating tables, scientists and physicians at work. Teams 2 and 3 arrived at the intersection just as Team 1 did. As they all stood in the center, they kept their eyes peeled for anything suspicious, the screen above them came to life.

"I'd like to introduce you to the head of our science division, Dr. Samuel Stoke!" The young woman stepped aside and a slightly younger Stoke stepped into frame.

"Hello. I understand this is a lot to take in, and it would only get more confusing if I tried to explain what exactly the M.O.R.S. Initiative is preparing, but I can assure you of one thing." The video seemed to skip a bit, as Stoke repeated the his last few words again and again until the picture cut out. Eventually, the video resumed, but now showed an active laboratory setting as an older Samuel Stoke stepped into frame. "Hello again. I'm glad you all made it."

"This isn't right Yoke, we need to move." Juliet didn't bother to look at Yoke while she spoke, instead she kept scanning the open spaces.

"What do you call yourself now? Is it Juliet?" Juliet turned and looked up at the television screen as Samuel Stoke began to laugh. "And you took the name of that janitor in Bosnia! That's rich!

"I'm not going to lie, I wish I were there in person to laugh in your face. If you're watching this, though, it means that in all likelihood, I'm dead. I knew your little ragtag group of friends weren't going to stop poking the beast, so I left some bread crumbs hoping you'd show up here." Juliet realized she had been scanned when they entered the facility, that set this video in motion. "Did you like the creepy little tour video? It was a failed concept that we almost moved forward with in the 90's.

"But hey, now you're here, and that means I get to play a little game with you. You see, after we couldn't get access to the necessary files regarding your little Albatross Unit pals, we decided we'd go after the families of some of your agency friends. So, if all went well, the children and spouses of some fairly important people within the F.B.I., the C.I.A., and the rest of them should have been gathered up and sent here for safe keeping.

"I always knew that my genetic experiments were always only a part of the overall M.O.R.S. plan, but they were fun to play with none the less. Mankind is going to see the next stage of its existence pretty soon, my friend, and I'm happy to have been a part of that. You, on the other hand, have caused nothing but problems since you escaped our Sarajevo branch. Our mutual friend, Dr. Issacs has desperately missed you. If you happen to make it out of here alive, I promise that you'll be seeing him very soon.

"But let's get back to the point of why you're here. The House of M.O.R.S. is sick of your meddling in our affairs. Clearly, if you've come here, you did not heed our warnings, you discarded our caveats, and you didn't think of the lives you were putting at risk. This is unless you've all personally outweighed the lives of these children and spouses by focusing on the big picture. If that is the case, well then I commend you for having the gall to show up. Either way, I'm glad you're here, because now I get to watch you play with all of our new little friends. So please, don't worry about rescuing them. I'd think saving your own skin would be more important right about now."

"Guys, I've got movement down the corridor!" Juliet turned around to see one of the agents from Team 2 pointing his rifle down the hallway. As the ceiling lights above continued to flicker, a little boy stood in the center of the hallway. "Target identified. He's name's Justin. He's the son of the Deputy Director of the NSA."

"Stay away from him!" Juliet pushed through the team as she watched the agent crouch down and step forward toward the boy. In between the flickers of light, Juliet could see the boy begin break into a spasm.

"We need some medical assistance here, this kid's having a seizure!" The agent rushed to the boy's side as Justin fell to the floor in a violent fit. The agent tried to hold him down as the boy's arms and legs thrashed back and forth. Juliet grabbed the agent by the collar and yanked him back. She scowled down at the agent for ignoring her warnings, and then turned back to the boy, aimed her rifle, and shot several rounds into his face. When the boy's body stopped flaying about and laid motionless on the floor, Juliet turned back to the group.

"What the hell was that? The boy was in shock!"

The agent pulled himself up off the floor and lunged at Juliet, only to be held back by Yoke. "Get off me! She just killed a kid!"

"You weren't there, in Nebraska, but you were briefed on this Agent! The boy was showing all the signs. We've been led into a trap! Like Stoke said, this is not a rescue mission. All contacts are to be considered hostile, whether they appear so or not. You got that?" Juliet grabbed the agent by the vest and brought him close to her, meeting his glare until he began to relax under her grip.

"Movement!"

"Shit, I've got movement over here too!"

"The mannequins! Target the mannequins!" Juliet looked at the nearest display case and watched as the mannequin dressed as a scientist began to convulse. These weren't mannequins, they were the kidnapped family members that were temporarily paralyzed and posed in costumes. This meant that each display room they had passed before were full of potential targets as well. She released the agent, stepped back and raised her rifle.

"Put them down before they have a chance to mutate!" The rest of the crew took positions, picked a target and opened fire. The space lit up in a blaze of glory until one by one the agents stopped firing. Juliet lowered her rifle in fear. The glass of each of the displays appeared to be bullet proof. Juliet stepped forward and examined the glass from floor to ceiling. "These glass panels are designed to be lowered into the floor. We don't have much time, we have to move."

One by one the hostages began to scream and shriek as the paralyzing agent wore off their vocal cords. Their convulsions became more and more violent as splats of blood painted the walls and glass. Their bones began to break, shift, while some pierced up through the skin and split, forming spikes all over the person's body. One man in his forties lunged toward the glass, pounding his fists on it, and begging for the nearby agent to help. The agent stepped back as the man's eyes exploded against the glass while his jaw dipped low and pulled away from his face.

"Where the hell do we go?" The agents were getting agitated as they watched the horrors unfold before them without any ability to make them stop.

"Yoke! It's you're call. Any moment now we'll be surrounded. Pick a corridor and let's go!" Yoke was stuck in a trance as he watched a helpless woman shed most of her skin, warp her bone structure, and triple her size as she transformed into a seven foot monster in less than a minute. Suddenly, the glass panels began to move, slowly lowering into the floor. Juliet grabbed Yoke by the arm and pulled him down Team 2's corridor as the space became filled with the roaring of beasts. "Everybody move! We gotta go now, Yoke! Run"

The team ran down the corridor, knowing full well that there were just as many display cases in front of them that were likely featuring the same nightmares as the ones behind them. Juliet found a terminal on the wall and called for the team to take defensive positions as she attempted to access it. Juliet entered some keystrokes to bring up the terminal's subcommands. When she bypassed it's subroutines, she launched a command prompt to connect with her systems. Once connected, Juliet began an internal search for the complete floor plans of the structure.

"I've got it. Let's move!" The team continued down the hallway as the roars behind them grew louder. "When we reach the next room there should be a door on the right that leads to a lower level."

"Do we really want to go deeper into this mess, Cubro?" Yoke didn't seem pleased with the idea.

"It's better than where we are now, Yoke. So get a move on!" Loud stomping and the scraping of metal could be heard from the intersection behind them. The creatures were advancing. The agents in the front of the group broke into a dead sprint down the hallway only to come to a screeching halt as they reached the open space.

"Oh shit!" The first agent out of the hallway was immediately snatched up by the giant claw of a ten foot tall monster as it ripped the agent in half and threw the lower part of his body deeper into the room next to a four foot tall creature that still had a shredded youth sized Batman shirt hanging around its neck. Each monster looked similar but slightly different. The bones that broke through their skin split off differently for each one. Some shed their human skin completely and walked around with an oozing outer layer of blood and muscle. All in all, each monster looked like a deformed version of its former human self, but with an immediate gain in size and weight as the new muscle and bone structures seemed to erupt from each of them.

"Open fire! Open fire!"

Streams of fire exploded across the room as the creatures converged on the group of agents. Juliet looked for their exit, but was distracted by one of the mutated children crawling across the ceiling toward the group. She fired several rounds toward the little monster, but it was too fast as it lunged from side to side before launching itself toward the group. The creature shrieked as it landed on the shoulders of one of the agents and immediately buried it's five inch long fangs into the agent's skull. Juliet fired upon the little demon, at close range, and didn't release the trigger until the bastard was shredded into pieces.

The large monster was blocking the way between the group of agents and their desired door. Three agents were firing full-auto into the beast's chest, but the bullets only seemed to dig a few inches deep. The beast lashed out it's talons and sliced one agent up into three vertical strips from his scrotum to his shoulders. Juliet knew it was only a matter of moments before they were attacked from behind as well, so she shoved passed the agent and dove to the ground beneath the monster. Pulling a grenade from her belt, Juliet pressed a release button that sprung two six inch mounting spikes out of the bottom.

Juliet dug the spikes deep into the meat of the monster's leg and then pulled the pin as she rolled out from underneath the beast. Diving out of the way, while simultaneously opening fire on two other monsters across the room, Juliet hit the glass covered floor and braced for impact. The grenade exploded, blowing off the monster's right leg and injuring his left. As it fell to the floor in pain, Juliet jumped on its back and dug her 9.25 inch saw top carbon steel blade deep into its skull.

"Get to the door, now!" Juliet and Yoke and two other agents laid down cover fire as the rest of the group ran for the door. One of the medium sized creatures sprung forward, ducking under the bullets and tackled one of the agents waiting to get through the door. The agent screamed as the beast came down on top of her and began pulling the woman apart, limb by limb. Juliet followed the remaining agents through the door and into the stairwell, then turned and slammed the door shut once Yoke and the last remaining agent made it through. There was no way to lock the door, so the three sprinted down the stairs to catch up with the group.

The stairwell went down three or four stories before another door was presented. Going through it, Juliet and the remaining fourteen agents headed down the hallway after moving some furniture to block the stairwell door. According to the maps, this hallway would lead to a large open hanger that had an escape hatch on the other side. Juliet raced to the end of the hall and pushed through a door into a large, dark, empty space. As she felt a breeze of sorts lick her neck, Juliet popped on her flashlight and scanned the wall until she found several large levers with little sun symbols above them.

As she began pulling down on each lever, Juliet heard the circuits click as large high bay dome lights began to pop on overhead. Juliet turned around to see something she had most certainly not expected; a cornfield, the size of two football fields. Looking to her left she saw a wheat field about the same size, and to her right what looked like Barley and Oat fields. All in all, the hanger stretched about a mile long and a couple hundred yards across, with high three story ceilings sporting hanging greenhouse bulbs.

"What is this place?" Yoke stood beside Juliet as they scanned the area.

"These are test crops. For what purpose, I don't know, but they were growing something down here other than corn." A loud bang resonated from down the hallway; the monsters had made it down the stairwell and were trying to break through the barrier. Juliet quickly returned to scanning the hanger until she found what looked like the door to the escape hatch on the other side of the field and four hundred yards or so down the way. "We've got to run. Now!"

The group began to sprint down the side of the field as Juliet tried to run as far as she could in the open to avoid getting lost in the crops. Within moments, numerous screeches and roars rang out from behind them as several creatures spilled into the hanger from the hallway. Juliet looked behind her to see the creatures temporarily stunned by the bright lights and open space before they began to notice the group a couple hundred yards away, and sprung into pursuit.

"Into the fields!" Juliet led the group into the corn fields as she attempted to run straight through to the other side. She could hear the pounding thuds of the larger creatures heading towards them at a remarkable speed and could only assume that the smaller ones could run much faster; like trying to outrun a horse. It seemed that the creatures did not recklessly abandon chunks of the human physic, but rather redistributed the muscles during the mutation to achieve highest efficiency as a predator. Some of them remained on two legs, like a humanoid, while others seemed more comfortable moving on four legs.

As astounding as it all was, Juliet could feel the monsters gaining on them. Looking behind her, Juliet watched as one of the smaller creatures sprung up on the back of one of the agents and pulled him down as a cheetah does an antelope. Juliet turned forward again, but not in time to notice the log on the ground, which tripped her and sent her flying head first into a sand pit. She scrambled to her feet, clutching her rifle in one hand and knife in the other as she looked up to realize she was standing in a large playground set up in the middle of the corn field. Juliet turned and realized they were not currently in a position to outrun the horde, and so she ran for the large metal fort with wooden accents and began climbing up the stairs to the first slide tower.

"Take defensive positions on the playground set! We have to stand our ground if we want to make it out of here alive." Juliet opened fire on the corn field as several agents broke into the clearing and rushed to climb up the playset. The fort was massive, enough to entertain a small park's worth of kids. Juliet thought if the team could secure high positions, they might have a shot at surviving. Yoke was one of the last to tumble out of the field and into the sand. Juliet could see two distinct movements within the field behind him as two smaller monsters appeared to be making a bee line for him. "Cover Yoke!"

The team opened fire into the field as they sprayed any stalk that moved with bullets until, eventually, they all ceased fire and waited for a sign of the creatures. There were no more creatures roaming the open side of the crops, and Juliet was not certain how many had poured into the hanger from the hall. All she knew for certain, was that they were out there, hiding within the density of the crops, waiting for an opportune time to strike. Juliet heard a stalk snap behind her and realized some of them must have circled around to the back of the playground as she turned just in time to see a medium size creature launch itself twenty feet across the sand to cling on to the side of the fort.

Juliet popped in her second to last magazine as she switched to three round bursts and started firing down upon the beast as it attempted to scale the side of the slide tower. Juliet focused on aiming at the creature's face, but it moved so quickly that few of her rounds hit their mark. The beast managed to climb about five feet from her before she shot two bursts into its head and watched it fall down to sand; motionless. A large beast rose out of the crops, likely because it had been crouched down on all fours, and charged the tower as two tiny creatures headed for the slides on either end. While one creature made it up the first slide and was ripping off the legs of the agent at the top, the other managed only to make it half way up the tall slide before Juliet clipped it.

The large monster rammed itself against the side of the playground structure, causing a few agents to fall off the other side. They had barely hit the sand for a second before several medium sized creatures broke onto the sand to retrieve them and drag them kicking and screaming back into the crops. Yoke was firing his weapon through the bars point blank into the chest of the large creature, covering himself in the monster's blood, but didn't seem to be doing anything but pissing it off more.

Juliet began firing at the side of its head as she tossed Yoke her last spike grenade. As the creature began to climb over the top rails of the fort, Yoke sprung the grenade spikes and dug it deep into the neck of the beast. The hulking abomination howled in pain as it swatted Yoke aside, sending him thirty feet in the air only to hit one of the railings on the way down and topple to the sand. The beast turned toward Juliet, but she quickly threw herself down the slide as the grenade exploded, tearing the giant apart.

As a couple of the agents still left on the structure provided cover fire, Juliet ran toward Yoke but was stopped short when two creatures sprung out of the crop field toward her direction. She didn't have time to scale the side of the fort, and wasn't near either of the ramps or ropes. At the last moment, she saw a metal cove underneath a lower lever metal walkway, digging through the sand just out of reach. Instead of following her under, the creatures simply landed on top of the walkway and attempted to grab her through the bars. Juliet sprayed the first beast in the face with several rounds of fire, but wasn't quick enough to avoid the second beast, as it's long craws swiped through the bars and dug into her stomach.

Juliet cried out in pain as she attempted to wiggle free. The creature showed its face against the bars, tried to force it threw enough to bite her, allowing Juliet an up-close look at it. She was surprised to see new eyeballs forming deep within the gaping puss filled sockets. The entirety of its epidermis was secreting blood, slime, and mucus at high temperatures as Juliet could see the actual steam rising off the creature's body. Juliet plunged her arm up and through the bars as she dug her knife into its eye socket and twisted it until the creature fell flat.

As she crawled out from under the playground, Juliet watched as Yoke was torn in two by two creatures fighting over his body. As several more beasts advanced on the fort, Juliet realized they were outmatched and outnumbered. She knew her visual feed was still streaming live back at base, and hoped they could hear her.

"Locke, just end it. Have the air base drop half a MOAB on this place, and burn it all to hell." Juliet loaded her last magazine and leaned against the bottom of the slide tower as she fired on anything that moved toward her. A MOAB (mother of all bombs) would set fire to everything within a mile radius, but one had never been dropped on American soil, let alone this close to a civilian population. Half a MOAB should do the trick. "Do it Locke. I might be able to get out of here, but don't wait."

As one creature climbed over the top of the fort and began scaling down the side toward Juliet, she quickly fired several rounds into its head causing it to crash down into the sand before her. As she wasted away the remainder of her ammo, she desperately searched through the bunker's systems to find an active link to a satellite dish or antenna on the surface. If she tried to teleport this deep underground, her signal might not make it through without assistance. As she heard a deafening thud hit the surface, she found an active high gain FM antenna and pressed her hand against the anchor tattoo on her forearm. In her final moments, Juliet felt the heat of the fireball reaching and engulfing the hanger in flames. Before she was burned alive, however, the teleporter activated and she was gone.

Joshua D. Howell

13 SIT TIGHT

SOMEWHERE

"Wake up, Agent Harper. This isn't a rehab facility. You aren't here to sleep-in and take mud baths." Riley opened her eyes to once again find herself strapped down to a vertical bed, but this time she wasn't alone in a dark closet. Instead, Riley was on display, in a wide open room, with little to no furniture save for a lab table set up to her left. The scientist at the table had his back to her, but she recognized his voice. As Dr. Timothy Hanes turned around, Riley tried not to laugh at his swollen lip. "I'm glad you find my pain amusing, Agent Harper. I will find yours equally amusing, when the time comes."

"Cut the shit, Hanes. Your voice was annoying in the breakroom, and remains just as annoying now.

So if you could do me a favor and skip the pleasantries, I'd appreciate it." Hanes stopped what he was doing, grabbed a scalpel, and walked over to Riley. With a quick flick of his wrist, Hanes sliced open Riley's left cheek, and then stood still and stared at her as she winced.

"This is important work we do here, Agent Harper. I will not be rushed." Hanes returned to his table as Riley felt the blood run down her cheek.

"I don't believe we've properly met, Tim. You know, I was good friends with your former superior, Samuel Stoke. I don't believe he ever mentioned you." Hanes raised his head a bit, as if Riley had struck nerve, but then went back to his work. "But look at you now, at the top of your science class. I guess all those years of being Stoke's bitch really paid off."

Hanes slammed his fist down on the table, causing a tray of tools to slip off the edge and fall to the floor with a clatter. Riley watched as Hanes took several visibly deep breathes before bending down to collect his fallen items. As he did so, a door opened at the far end of the room and in walked a woman in her fifties, escorted by two armed guards. The woman with her hair slicked back was dressed in a black skirt, a long sleeved purple dress shirt, and high heels that echoed with each step deeper into the large empty room.

"Good morning, Ms. Harper. You look well." The woman smiled as she grabbed the one chair in the room and dragged it to a position a few feet in front of Riley. "Have you been fed?"

"She ate my damn sandwich last night! The bitch can starve for all I care." Hanes apparently seemed to still be holding a grudge. The woman rolled her eyes and signaled one of the guards behind her.

"You. Get Ms. Harper something fresh from the chow hall, but keep it light as she hasn't ingested much solid food in the past few weeks." The guard power walked out of the room and the woman returned her attention to Riley. "My apologies for some of our more crass staff. Tensions get a little high when you're underground for long periods of time. Also, the lower levels really do value their food labeling system."

"My bad. I guess I should have looked harder for the container with my name on it." Hanes grunted, but the woman just smiled and kept her composure. "Why am I alive?"

"Because we kept you alive, Ms. Harper. Just

because we are enemies, doesn't mean I can't recognize you as a formidable opponent. Had my hitman successfully killed you in that asbestos infected motel in Maine, I would have considered you nothing more than a nosey redhead who couldn't mind her own business." The woman leaned forward and grinned. "But you didn't die. You went on to form a band of oddballs and managed to expose our operations in Nebraska. Even though we cleared out that facility before your team had a chance to infiltrate, I was still impressed you made it that far.

"But you didn't stop there. Even after we sent your little boy toy to Langley to officially warn you, you still kept going! You actually went down to Panama! I was there one afternoon cleaning up Samuel's mess and I despised it, but you were there for six months! I had hoped to meet you in person when I raided your little makeshift safe house, but you evaded me there as well.

"Riley, I brought the entire freaking building down on top of you, and you still didn't call it a day. Moments later you were hauling ass after me to the point where I had to call in the Calvary to take care of you." The woman chuckled as she sat back and took out a piece of gum from her pocket. Popping it in her mouth, she smiled once again and then shook her head. "No, no, no. When my guy had you dead to rights on the concrete there in the middle of the highway, I couldn't just have him kill you right then! You made it this far! Who was I to deny you a chance to see how it all ends? No, I couldn't do that. So, I brought you back here to my little abode and had you fixed up."

"For what purpose? Am I your trophy now? The latest in your list of victories? I'm no good to you as a hostage. Albatross will not bargain for me, or bow down to any demands in exchange for my life." Riley watched out of the corner of her eye as Hanes continued to fiddle with his things on the table. "And if you're planning on injecting me with the same shit you gave Peter, you should just get it over with. I've seen what it does. There's a chance I'll be just fine, or my body will explode with little spikes, or I'll turn into one of your little monsters and try to kill everyone in this room. Place you bets and roll the dice. I'm tired of waiting."

"Oh no, dear, we aren't going to inject you with that silly stuff. I don't care one way or the other whether your compatible or not. Hanes, here, is just making me an incredibly elaborate cocktail using only his little chemistry set. This is his punishment for allowing you to get the better of him in the lounge." The far door opened as the guard returned with a tray of food. "Ah good, your food is here."

"And the guard? What did you make him do? One hundred pushups?" The woman laughed a bit.

"No, dear. We killed him. Disposable help should always be reminded how disposable they really are." Hanes finally turned around as he poured some liquid from a measuring flask into a cocktail glass and handed it to the woman. "Thank you, Hanes. Now clean your shit up and leave Ms. Harper to eat in peace."

"I'm not hungry, and I'm low on patience." One of the guards laid Riley back as he locked the bed back into a horizontal position, and then began to unstrap her restrains. After he removed all of the straps, the guard handcuffed Riley to a bar on the side of the bed, and helped her sit up as he placed her plate on the bed beside her.

"Well you're going to have to wait just a little bit longer, Ms. Harper." The woman stood up and smoothed out her skirt. "It won't be too long though, I swear. Soon this world will be unrecognizable, and you will have the opportunity to thank me for giving you shelter from the storm. So sit tight, and eat up."

14 THERE'S BLOOD ON THE IVORY

TENNESSEE

Secretary of State Lisa Pennet leaned against the back wall of her barn, smoking a Black and Mild while she tried to stop her hands from shaking. What had she gotten herself into? She thought this was just another form of elitism, an under the table membership that could help her career in the long run. She certainly didn't expect to see her dollars at work on CNN with a label of global terrorism attached as a shadowy figure from the nightmare factory threatened the end of the world as she knew it. The news stations had analyzed that broadcast backwards and forwards, twenty-four seven, for the past few weeks and she couldn't take it anymore. She took a long pull from the cigar as she began to pace back and forth.

They had given her a phone number, in fact, one morning she just found it programmed into her phone with just one letter attached to it. She had never dialed the number, and knew that she was never supposed to, but now her thumb was hovering over the call button. She was disgusted with herself. On one hand, she knew that her public persona would immediately denounce this organization and everything it stood for. Outside of the public eye, standing alone next to four empty horse stables, she could only tremble in fear and take some kind of comfort knowing that she had made the cut and secured a spot on a list somewhere to be spared from whatever was about to come. Still, she had no idea what that impending doom really was. If not nuclear war, then what could possibly wipe out the human existence without harming her and her own in the process?

She wanted answers, she needed answers. Even if it was a lackey, or some low-level assistant with M.O.R.S., she wanted someone to scream at, to plead with, to listen to her vent and provide her some assurances. This is not what she had signed up for, and being kept out of the loop, alone in the dark with no sense of who else on Capitol Hill had also paid for their name to be on the list, was incredibly unnerving.

"Dinner is ready, sweetheart." Lisa took another drag as her husband called from the back porch. She dropped the cigar down into the dirt and stomped it out with her boot as she popped in some gum and headed for the house. Before she could make it out of the barn, however, she suddenly realized that her husband had called her sweetheart. She despised that name. Her husband had dated his 'high school sweetheart' for years before they broke up and he settled for her. Lisa had told him the word made her feel like second place. She despised it so much, in fact, that she had told him to only call her that if he needed to signal that something was wrong.

Lisa resumed walking toward the house, looking up at the windows, but seeing nothing that immediately struck her as off. Still, she stopped by the tree on the way to the back porch, reached up into the tree hole about six feet from the ground, and grabbed the handgun that she had stashed inside. Pressing her index finger against the recognition slab, she deactivated and removed the trigger lock, and continued toward the house. After verifying her ammo and cocking the hammer, Lisa gently mounted the stairs of the back porch and creeped toward the back door.

Peering into the house, she saw her husband being gagged and forced down to his knees to be tied up next to their teenage daughter and seven-year-old son. Lisa may not have been trained in tactical assaults, but she had known how to shoot a gun since her dad taught her in 3rd grade, and she would be damned if she didn't defend her family. Just as she was about to pull open the door, however, she heard a wooden plank creek to her right. She turned in time to see a figure lunge at her. She fired off a shot at the man's head, but it only ricocheted off as the man came into the light, swatted away her gun, and slammed her against the house. Lisa screamed as the light revealed the man's head to be a dirty skull, staring back at her while a skeleton hand gripped her by the throat.

"Good evening, Secretary Pennet." Lisa screamed again at the sound of the man's creepy distorted voice. Even though she knew the skull was a mask, it did not bring her any comfort as the dark eye sockets seemed to stare into her soul. "My name is Mr. Bones. Why don't we go inside and have a chat."

Mr. Bones picked up Lisa's handgun from the floor of the porch and then pulled her to the door. Opening it, he pushed her into the house, past her family on their knees in the dining room, and down the hall to the living room. There were several men in the house, all concealed by black masks, holding different assault rifles and standing guard. Lisa heard her daughter whimper behind her as Mr. Bones shoved her down onto a wooden chair. As one of the other men began zip tying her wrists and ankles to the chair, Mr. Bones casually strolled across the living room and let his boney fingers run over the black and white keys of the family piano; playing an eerie tune.

"This piano looks to be at least fifty or sixty years old, and yet the keys look to be in pristine condition; ivory keys in fact." Mr. Bones looked over at the Secretary as he continued to drag his fingers over the keys. "Did you import some fresh elephant tusks to rejuvenate the family keepsake? Brutal!

"But I'm not here to discuss your tastes for slaying wildlife so your little brats can play chopsticks. No, unfortunately I'm here to discuss your association with an organization who recently committed to destroying the planet. Now you may not care much for big African game, but one would think a person in your political office would care about the innocent lives currently being threatened by the people you gave money to." Lisa shook her head and began to sob.

"I didn't know, I swear! I didn't know this was going to happen! I didn't!" Mr. Bones picked up a vase of freshly cut flowers and threw it against the wall next to Lisa, causing it to shatter and send debris flying everywhere including some smaller pieces that dug into the side of her neck and face.

"Liar!" Mr. Bones turned to the men in the dining room. "Take the family out back and get them ready!"

"No! Leave my family alone!" Lisa screamed and sobbed as she struggled against the zip ties and the chair, but it was no use as she watched her husband and children get dragged out of the house. She turned back to Mr. Bones. "They're innocent! You can't hurt them, they didn't do anything!"

"Oh I am sick of hearing the same shit over and over again from you people! My family is innocent! Don't hurt them! They didn't do anything!" Mr. Bones nodded at the man standing next to the Secretary. She looked up at the man as he quickly removed his M9 from its holster and shot her once in her left bicep. As Lisa screamed out in pain, Mr. Bones approached her, grabbed her by the arms and pressed his skull against her face. "What about the rest of the world, Secretary? What about their families?

"While you're screaming you little head off about a mere flesh wound, millions of families around the world are living in fear, not knowing what the House of M.O.R.S. has planned for them." Mr. Bones released her and stepped back, putting his hands on his hips and looking down at the piano. "Oh shoot, now there's blood on the ivory. Well, listen, perhaps you're right. Perhaps your family is innocent in all of this, and their lives should be spared. So, I'm going to give you a chance to save them. Tell me something valuable about the House of M.O.R.S., and I won't order my men to shoot your husband."

"Please! I told you! I don't know anything. I just gave them some money! I don't know where it went! I swear on my life, I don't know anything!"

"Unfortunately, your life is not the one currently in question, Secretary. Now you're going to have to watch your husband die." Mr. Bones walked behind Lisa, grabbed the back of her chair and began dragging her back down the hallway and into the dining room. Mr. Bones released the chair beside a large window pane, and then bent down to press Lisa's face against the glass. "Are you ready, Secretary?"

"No! Please don't, I told you I don't know anything." Lisa sobbed against the glass as she saw a man position himself behind her husband.

"Do it!"

"NO!" Lisa cried out against the glass as she watched the man fire one round into her husband's back. As his body fell to the ground, Lisa's husband stopped moving and laid dormant next to his two weeping children. Lisa shoved herself off the window, and turned to Mr. Bones. "How could you?! How could you!? You psychopath! Why would you do that? Why?! WHY?!"

"Calm her down." Mr. Bones said to a nearby masked man who then promptly slapped her across the face. Mr. Bones sat down in an open chair next to Lisa and stared at her. "I'm glad to see the pain in your face, Secretary. It tells me that you aren't so heartless after all. But I have to tell you, even though my man pulled the trigger back there, that shot was on your hands. Just as the death and destruction that reigned down upon this country is on your hands as well. Now, I don't think you're some mastermind for M.O.R.S., but I think that there's something you could tell me about them. If you tried really hard."

"Please. Stop this!" Lisa looked up and pleaded with Mr. Bones, staring into the place holes of his face. "If you care at all for human life, then please…"

"Do the boy next." Mr. Bones stood up from the chair, clearly dissatisfied at Lisa's response.

"No! You leave my son alone!" Lisa screamed

over and over again, but it was no use. With her bleeding face pressed once again against the glass, Lisa watched in horror as the triggerman stepped past Lisa's daughter and fired a round into the back of her son. "NO! Oh God no! No!"

"Oh God no? Oh God no? Secretary, I hate to break it to you, but I don't think God is currently concerned with the wellbeing of a mass murderer's family members." Mr. Bones looked up at the ceiling and stared at it for a moment. "Then again, I could be wrong. Honestly, God and I haven't had much in terms of private conversations as of late."

"You bastard! You evil, self-righteous bastard! I hope you die a horrible death! I hope the House of M.O.R.S. kills your whole damn family, and I hope they rot in hell!" Mr. Bones grabbed Lisa by the throat and leaned in close to her.

"Oh, my family's already dead, sweetheart. Come to think of it, they're likely rotting in hell as we speak. So you're going to have to do better than that!" Mr. Bones shoved Lisa's face back against the window. "Now I saved your oldest for last, because we all know how mommies love their daughters! So, here's your last chance to save her, Secretary. Tell me something, anything, and I'll let her live."

"I... I don't....I can't...please, I can't."

Suddenly, Mr. Bones let go of Lisa and brought her back from the window.

"Wait, what did you just say? You can't? YOU CAN'T? Have you been holding out on me, Secretary? This whole time you've been risking the lives of your family over some far-fetched fear of what M.O.R.S. might do to you if you speak?" Lisa stared up at him through her tears, unable to come up with something to say. "Oh you selfish bitch! I knew it! Shoot the girl!"

Lisa wailed and cried as she turned to see the gunman shoot her daughter in the back. As her chair was dragged back down the hall, Lisa struggled to get one last look at the bodies of her loved ones lying motionless in the mud. Lisa's chair was brought back to the living room as Mr. Bones took a hammer to the keys of the family piano, sending shards of black and white ivory flying across the room.

"I'll break every bone in your body, I swear to you I'll do it!" Mr. Bones hit the keys with every word, driving his point home. Lisa felt sick as she struggled to breathe amidst her tears. She stared at the floor as she caught her breath, allowing the death of her children, of her husband, to sink in.

"She was an old friend of mine from college." Mr. Bones stopped smashing the piano and turned around abruptly to listen to the Secretary as she sobbed. "I hadn't seen her in years, but she showed up to my firm with a proposition. She said she could put me on a path toward a position with the State Department. She said she had stumbled onto something massive, and it was going to change the world in a couple of decades."

"You knew her?"

"Yes, and I trusted her, but I could see the ambition in her eyes and knew that it wasn't necessarily something for the good of all people. She was always a radical thinker, even if she had kept it to herself most of the time." Lisa sobbed as she sucked in the tears flowing from her eyes. "Before I knew it, I was waist deep in it all, with no way out. I didn't know the true scale of it until the broadcast, but I knew the danger I would be in if I tried to step away. So I kept my mouth shut, and hoped whatever happened was something I could eventually learn to live with; so long as my family was safe. Oh God, my family!"

"Tell me her name, Secretary!" Mr. Bones grabbed Lisa by the jaw and forced her to look at him. "Tell me the woman's name!"

"I can't, dammit! She'll kill me!"

"I'll kill you!" Mr. Bones reached inside his suit jacket and pulled out a silver plated pistol and aimed it at Lisa's forehead. "I will kill you right now, if you don't!"

"Do it! I've got nothing else, just do it!" Lisa began openly sobbing and screaming again.

"Give me the name! The name, Secretary! Tell me!" Mr. Bones tried to raise his voice louder than her screams, but it was no use. He considered firing a round into one of her legs, and was about to pull the trigger before he heard it, a ringing sound coming from the kitchen; the Secretary's cellphone. "Get the phone!"

One of his men ran into the kitchen and fished the phone out of the Secretary's purse. Running it back to the living room, the gunman tossed it to Mr. Bones as he looked down at the caller ID. The previous phones he had gathered had a restricted number with the letter "M" attached to it, but Mr. Bones had failed to trace the numbers back to anywhere. The letter on the Secretary's caller ID, however, read "R" instead. It kept ringing and ringing until Mr. Bones eventually slid the icon over to accept the call. Putting the phone on speaker, Mr. Bones waited for the other party to speak first. The initial moment of silence was deafening.

"Mr. Bones, I assume?" An older female voice rang out from the phone. Mr. Bones looked up at the Secretary, who had a shocked look on her face. "This is Mr. Bones, isn't it?"

"Yes. Who is this?"

"My name is not important. What is important is that you realize how much the House of M.O.R.S. does not appreciate you killing our friends."

"Perhaps you should have thought of that before roping them into your sadistic plans for world destruction." Mr. Bones looked out the window, checking for signs of an approaching force, but didn't see anything.

"Touché, Mr. Bones. Either way, I'm going to need you to leave Secretary Pennet's house right now, or suffer the consequences." Mr. Bones motioned for his men to take defensive positions. He looked down at the Secretary once more, then back at the phone.

"I'm afraid I can't do that. The Secretary was just about to share with me some information too valuable to pass up." Lisa sobbed loudly at Mr. Bones' response.

"I see. Well then you've given me no other choice. Goodbye Mr. Bones, and goodbye Lisa."

The line went dead, and the room fell quiet. Mr. Bones looked out the window again, but saw nothing but darkness. Then he heard something faint in the distance. Lisa began to cry again, but Mr. Bones quickly covered her mouth.

"Shut up! Shut up!" Mr. Bones listened for the sound again, and then realized in horror what it was as it rapidly sounded closer and louder. "Everybody take cover!"

A bright light suddenly shined through the bay window of the living room as an RAH-66 Comanche Stealth attack helicopter lowered into view. Mr. Bones could hear the whirring of the 30mm hydraulically driven seven-barreled Gatling-gun style cannon, mounted on the underbelly of the helicopter, as it prepared to fire. The helicopter opened fire, as the house was sprayed with a earsplittingly loud continuous stream of bullets. With the capability of firing up to 4,200 rounds per minute, the cannon proceeded to obliterate everything in its path. Mr. Bones watched through the debris as Lisa's body was torn to shreds by several rounds of fire, leaving nothing behind that could be recognizable. Mr. Bones crawled down the hallway as the walls splintered and exploded around him. Reaching the back door, he sprung to his feet and sprinted off the back porch.

As Mr. Bones ran past the unconscious bodies of Lisa's family, each lying on the ground with a single tranquilizer dart sticking out of their backs, he motioned for his men to head towards the woods. As he passed the barn, Mr. Bones looked behind him to see the attack collapse the house in on itself as the helicopter advanced over the fallen structure and resumed fire toward his fleeing men.

"Get to the trees!" Mr. Bones ran as fast as he could while simultaneously trying to see through the darkness of the country side. His only hope was that the helicopter couldn't follow them into the forest, and that some of them might survive if they could get in deep and hide. As Mr. Bones ran past the tree line and into the woods, he heard the helicopter's cannon tear through the barn and then through the first line of trees. He looked to his left as several of his men were mowed down by the stream of fire. This was not good.

The trees around him splintered into pieces as Mr. Bones ran for his life. The helicopter, now firing down from above the trees, seemed to be firing continuously at random into the forest, as it probably couldn't get a clear shot. Mr. Bones counted his blessings as he approached a small slope and jumped over the edge.

As he scaled down the steep woodland slope, he

saw what appeared to be a road at the bottom of it. Looking to his left, Mr. Bones saw a truck barreling down the road at high speeds, honking it's horn. As the helicopter circled overhead, taking out several more of his men, Mr. Bones launched himself again down the slope, attempting a controlled fall of some sort. After colliding with some thick brush and just missing a fallen tree by a foot or so, Mr. Bones came rolling to a stop at the edge of the road. The truck swerved to a stop beside him, and the passenger door was kicked open.

"Get in!" Mr. Bones looked up to see the face of Juliet Cubro looking down at him from the driver's seat. Scrambling to his feet, Mr. Bones climbed into the truck and shut the door as Juliet kicked it into high gear and took off down the road. Mr. Bones looked at the side mirror to see the helicopter take notice of the truck and turn to pursue it.

"It's coming around! We have to go faster!"

"We've gotta get off this road." The truck swerved to the right and ran off the road onto a forest path that looked like it could have been a service road at some point. Juliet plowed down the road a ways before slamming on the breaks and bringing the truck to a halt. "Get out and find some cover!"

As Mr. Bones leapt from the truck and dove into the brush, Juliet opened up the back door and pulled a case out of the truck and onto the ground. Unsnapping the case, she threw open the lid to reveal an RPG-7 Anti-Tank rocket launcher. As the helicopter reached the service road entrance from the main road and turned in to follow, Juliet loaded the RPG and crouched down into the brush. The helicopter grew closer as the cannon started up again, causing a stream of fire to dig into the dirt toward the truck. When the helicopter was in range, Juliet pulled the trigger and then ran for cover.

The PG-7VM 70-mm HEAT rocket launched into the air and flew towards its target. After penetrating the outer hull of the helicopter, the rocket detonated, blasting a large hole in the side of the helicopter and breaking off a part of its tail. The cannon continued to fire sporadically, digging bullets into the ground, the trees, and the brush as the stealth helicopter spun out of control for a few moments only to crash into the forest a few hundred yards away. As a mass ball of fire rose up through the trees from the crash site, Mr. Bones rose up from his hiding spot and looked for his rescuer. After a moment, Juliet rose from the brush and started making her way back to the truck with the RPG in hand. Mr. Bones did the same, but stopped when he reached the road. Juliet dropped the RPG and walked over to him.

"Are you alright?" Juliet stared at him, compassion in her eyes.

"I'm fine, thank you. Are you?" Mr. Bones stared back, wondering where to go from there.

"We have to leave before any reinforcements arrive." Juliet loaded the RPG and then climbed into the driver's seat. Mr. Bones got in on the passenger side and buckled up.

"Thank you, for saving me." Juliet turned the engine over and looked back at Mr. Bones, hearing the sincerity of his appreciation.

"You're welcome, Gene."

15 THIRST

KENTUCKY

"How long have you known?" Eugene sat at the table, the skull mask sitting next to him.

"That you were Mr. Bones? I knew almost immediately. I could tell that you were getting bored with your leash at Albatross." Juliet handed Eugene a drink and then sat down across from him. "How did you keep it a secret from Locke?"

"After I found the cameras, I immediately installed my own to record, edit, and then loop based on the time of day. I recorded several hours' worth of video, with different clothes, doing different activities, and then plugged them into an app on my phone. Synced that up with Albatross' network, and done. When I went out, I pressed play and they were none the wiser." Juliet smiled.

"You were always clever. Though I don't think Locke would be too happy to learn the truth."

"For all of our secrecy and authority, Albatross is still held back by some kind of standard. Locke is trapped behind too much red tape. As a consultant, I'm not." Eugene took a sip and sighed as he looked around the place. "*Balvenie*, 14 year old, *Caribbean* Cask whisky, my favorite. Your loft is in L.A., isn't it? What's this place?"

"One of many small places I have around the country, if I ever need a place to lie low." Eugene stood up and walked around the place. It was much smaller than Juliet's main loft, at least from what he could tell off the Albatross feeds. On the wall opposite the table was a large bookshelf, full of literary pieces from all over the world. Eugene searched around until he found the book he was looking for, Romeo and Juliet.

"Is this….?"

"Yes. That's the book from Edin's apartment." Eugene opened it to find a picture of a middle-aged man, holding a mop, wearing a University of Sarajevo polo; he was smiling. "That's him, before he started working at the facility."

"You knew I was listening in on your talk with

Locke?"

"I did."

"I could tell there was more to the story, between the time Edin passed and you showing up in my home." Eugene sat back down in his chair and took another sip. "You wanna finish it?"

"Yes." Juliet finished her glass of rum, and poured herself some more. "The scientist assigned to me was Dr. Timothy Hanes. Hanes was capable, for sure, but he was a hot head and liked to mix work with pleasure. He had a grudge against Samuel Stoke from the start, as he thought he should have been higher on the totem pole than Stoke. Stoke would visit the facility from time to time, and check in on our progress. He spoke to me personally on several occasions to test my speech and other skills. The fact was, neither Stoke nor Hanes invented any of the technology used to make me who I am, or half of the other things the M.O.R.S. Initiative dabbles with. They were given the tools and taught how to use them, and then they went from there.

"Hanes may not have liked working under Stokes' thumb, but he certainly liked other parts of his job. I wasn't the only child that was grown in the facility. I also wasn't the only girl chosen to be a sex toy. This is how M.O.R.S. secured so many of their donors and friends in high places; they either created personal slaves, like what I was supposed to be, or they created clones that could be used as organ donors for the rich and old.

"Hanes was known for field testing his work. Late in the night, he would 'break in' the new girls before they were to be shipped to their owner. He had his eyes on me from the very beginning. Every time I would get caught sneaking out of the facility, he would remind me that one day he was going to have his way with me, and that I wouldn't like it. When it was official that I would be turned into a mindless doll for someone to play with, Hanes let me know that my last night at the facility would be eventful, and that I would be lucid for all of it.

"When the night came, my last night, I was woken from my sleep, stripped naked, and strapped down to a gurney. When I tried to scream in protest, Dr. Hanes' assistant, Dr. Malcom Palmer, muted my vocals. I remember him looking down at me, telling me he was sorry. He left me in a dark room for a few moments, and then Dr. Hanes came in. I could smell the alcohol in his sweat and could see the cocaine on the edges of his nostrils.

"He was laughing as he ran his hands over me, admiring his work. He told me that he had waited for this moment since I was born, and that for all my trouble, he was not going to dampen my cognitive functions until after it was all over. He said there was no fun in taking something from a lifeless being; he preferred when they struggled. He shed his clothes and climbed on top of me, howling like a rabid dog as he held me down. It was at that moment that a flashbang grenade ignited in the room, and group of men rushed in to pull Hanes off of me.

"They had a picture of me, the one that Edin took. When I nodded, they quickly wrapped me in a blanket, and pulled me down the hallway. They told me that they were a local militia, left over from the Cold War, and that Edin had contacted them to rescue me. I could tell they were a bit in over their heads with this attack on the facility, but it was after hours, and they had the manpower to raid the facility. I knew that this rescue was pointless, however, if the facility could just recall me the next day.

"I broke free of them and ran to the line of hostages being watched in the hall. I grabbed Dr. Palmer by the throat and motioned for him to unmute me. After he did so, I told him that he would die that night if he did not assist me. While my rescuers followed Dr. Palmer to collect his things, I ran back to kill Dr. Hanes. When I reached the room, he was already gone, and I knew we didn't have the time to search for him. I grabbed some scrubs from a closet and left with the militia. We managed to take a complete teleporter unit, 10 boxes of necessities, and a flash drive containing the bulk of Dr. Palmer and Dr. Hancs' work. The militia lost several men on our way out, but we did make it out, and once we got deep into Sarajevo, we went underground where it was safe.

"It was only then that I was told of Edin's death. Edin's cousin, Aldin, was in the militia, and although he had never shared his cousin's ambitions for war, Edin had remained on good terms with Aldin. When Edin went missing, Aldin knew that the worst had likely happened. By this time, Edin's apartment had been ransacked and cleared out, leaving not one thing behind for Edin's loved ones. Edin had mailed the book of Romeo and Juliet, with a photograph, to Aldin to keep for me.

"We held a funeral for Edin on a hilltop outside of the city. With no body to bury, we simply mourned over an empty grave, and shared memories. Mine were short, but I cherished them above all. Edin was the first kind person I ever met that wasn't being paid to be kind. His intentions were transparent, and his compassion was overwhelming. When I was being rescued, I had simply assumed that Edin would be waiting back in the city for me. I never once thought of a life outside of the facility that didn't involve him. He was the closest thing I would ever have to a fatherly figure, and I didn't really get the chance to say goodbye. I swore I would avenge him, but at that point I wasn't ready to do so.

"Over the next few months, I focused on two things. The first was to force Dr. Palmer to teach me everything he knew about how the teleporter worked, about the max efficiency of my abilities, and whatever he knew about the men who ran the facility. Palmer reprogrammed my network to keep M.O.R.S. from forcing me back, and showed me how I could track down and infiltrate other facilities. The second thing was to learn as much about combat from the militia as I could; weapons training, fighting, and so on. While Palmer didn't know much about the heads of M.O.R.S., he confirmed that Reynolds Pharmaceuticals supplied many of the supplements I had taken over the years, and that they worked hand in hand with Samuel Stoke and Timothy Hanes.

"Stoke and Hanes were off the grid, but your family wasn't. While your mother had passed, your father was still operating the philanthropy division at Reynolds, and I saw that as my in. The landlord of Edin's building was able to tell Aldin enough of a description for us to determine who attacked and killed Edin. We tracked down Mr. Hendricks at a dive bar, and I took my revenge; whispering into his ear that this was for Edin Cubro, while stabbing a knife deep into each of his ears.

"Dr. Palmer remained useful over the next six months, as he secured my way into America, and helped me set up a functioning teleporter unit in my L.A. loft. He made lists of everything I needed to sustain the machine for years to come. Once we cashed out his bank account, I castrated him with a steak knife, slit his throat, and left him in a dumpster on the docks. It wasn't long after, that I began my plan to infiltrate your family. I learned of the summer internship, and applied for it. Aldin and his militia had created an identity for me back in Sarajevo, and even had contacts at the University that forged my diploma and history there. I found out the name of the man responsible for picking the lucky winner, and had some foreign professionals threaten the lives of him and his family if he did not choose their cousin, the female applicant from Sarajevo.

"And you know the rest from there." Juliet downed the rest of her glass and leaned back in her chair. "I actually figured you'd be in that private school for another year, and didn't expect you to be home. I never saw you as a target, but I also never planned on getting to know you either. I didn't plan on your kindness, or you interest. You caught me off guard on my first major assignment, and I almost considered not going through with it because of you."

"All that time that I hated you. All those years planning to kill you. All that self-pity I drowned myself in, when my loss could never have compared to the things you went through." Eugene poured himself some more Balvenie . "And then thinking you'd left me to rot in my hatred and self-pity, when all along you were still keeping eyes on me."

"I knew you needed space, but then when you checked yourself into Summerhill, I thought I could at least watch your back from there. While you were still being housed separately from the general population, I posed as a humanitarian wanting to remodel Summerhill's dayroom. I donated a sizable sum to have it modernized. During the nights, with the room sectioned off and no one around, I snuck in and personally installed a second teleportation unit there in case of an emergency. I put the bulk of the unit in the ceiling, and made the platform into a large black circle in the middle of the room. I told the warden that it was some modern Zen thing to encourage peace and tranquility within Summerhill."

"I never deserved any of the things you did for me."

"But you did things for me too. I had not intended to stay as long as I did at your family's home. I wanted your father dead, so I could move on to the next target. But you surprised me, and intrigued me, and I found that I could be a normal girl with you; normal being so far from what I really was. I longed to be with you, to please you, and to see your eyes when you smiled. I was absolutely infatuated with you."

"But you couldn't betray your mission."

"No, I couldn't. I was filled with so much rage the night I killed your father. Rage more for the sake of knowing that I had to kill him, and that I would have to leave you once I did. I had planned to do it differently, and not in a way that would frame you. Before you were acquitted, I was planning to break you out of jail, and extradite you to some place safe where you could start over."

"You had a plan for everything, didn't you." Eugene smiled as he sipped some more.

"You were the first person, outside of a father figure, that I had ever fallen in love with. You made me feel safe and yet vulnerable at the same time. I needed so much to do right by you. I'm sorry it took so long to accomplish that, Gene."

"You have nothing to apologize for." Eugene reached across the table and took Juliet's hand in his. "I promise you, you don't. It is I who owe you a debt. All the things you did for me, and at the end of it all, I still kept my distance because of my own insecurities."

"I never blamed you."

"I know, but I blamed myself." The two looked at each for a long moment, drinking in the silence between them. Finally, Juliet pulled back her hand and rose up from her seat. Putting her glass in the sink, she turned a light on for the back hallway.

"There's a spare bedroom at the end of the hall. Everything should be good to go in there. I'm going to take a shower and get some sleep." Juliet walked down another hallway to the master bedroom and bath. "Goodnight, Gene. I'm glad you're safe."

"Goodnight."

Eugene sat in the dark, drink in hand, at a loss for words. He had not been prepared for the things that Juliet had described, the trials she had gone through. When he first saw her, naked in his bathroom, he had no idea who she was, or what she had endured to get here. When he had spent nights out with her, beneath the city lights, he had never sensed the pain that must have been boiling beneath her skin. When he saw her, with the knife, killing the last family member he had, he didn't see her pain for what it was; he refused to. As he sat now, in the dark of her living room, after being rescued by her hand for a third time, he felt the weight of his mistakes overtake him.

****

Juliet stood in the shower, leaning against the rock wall under the warm water, drowning herself in her thoughts as the steam fogged up the glass door. She worried that she had dumped too much on Eugene, that she had revealed more than she should have. If Eugene had been hesitant about her before, Juliet feared that adding more blocks to the fire would only seal his reservations in place. She still loved him, and no drug or liquor, club or house party, empty or full bed could change that. She would always love him, even if she was alone in that venture. Her eyes opened to a knock on the shower door. She opened it to Eugene standing there, looking at the floor.

"I should have never let you go." Eugene looked

up at her, locking in her eyes with his. "I'm still incredibly in love with you, and I don't want to pretend, any longer, like there's a reason that I shouldn't be."

Juliet almost stumbled as she stepped out of the water to meet him. Eugene placed a hand on her cheek and kissed her deeply as he pulled her into him with his other arm. The texture of his lips had never changed, not since the last time they kissed at Albatross, nor since the last kiss from their last date when he was younger. But this kiss was different. No longer did Juliet sense a reserve in Eugene or an uncertainty that stood like a wall between them. Instead, Eugene kissed her with abandon, and she was engulfed in his passion.

Within moments she had shed his clothes and pulled him into the shower with her. The water could have been ice cold, and she wouldn't have noticed because of the heat that radiated off of Eugene. His hands roamed her body as if he were blind and trying to memorize ever curve and plateau of her figure by touch. His lips kissed her lips, her cheek, her jaw and neck; drinking in her skin as if an unquenchable thirst had overtaken him. Juliet had longed for this moment for years to the point that she almost forgot to participate, feeling content to allow Eugene to take her without restriction or restraint. For she belonged to him, and always had belonged to him; from their first date, she had committed herself to him, and him alone. Finally, after all the years of trying to trying to fill a hole within her with empty pleasures, she now knew what it meant to feel whole.

When their initial moments of exploratory desire passed, Juliet found herself staring into Eugene's eyes as he became one with her. He held her against the wall as she wrapped her legs around him, and the two began to breathe in sync with one another. With each breath, Juliet felt his strength within, rippling through every inch of her, filling her with oxygen as if she her lungs had been inert all this time. She inhaled his passion and exhaled her satisfaction as she pressed herself against him, yearning for his warmth. She kissed him, profoundly and profusely, and begged for him not to stop, not to release her, and never to leave her.

****

Eugene stared at the ceiling in the dark of Juliet's room as she cuddled against him beneath the sheets. He smiled as he held her, knowing that this was likely the first thing he had done right in a very long time. Submerged in a bliss that he had never yet known, Eugene closed his eyes and let it overtake him. He had denied himself this overwhelming peace for far too long, and was happy to be held hostage by it now.

"Thank you again for saving me."

"Of course. Though I have to give it to you. The balls you had to take out the Secretary of State, all on a hunch that she might know something." Juliet placed her chin on Eugene's chest. "I'm guessing she didn't have anything useful to say."

"Holy shit!" Eugene sat up in bed, realizing he had forgotten everything that Pennet had said due to the urgency of running for his life. He leapt off the bed and grabbed his pants off the floor, retrieving the Secretary's phone from his front pocket. "How could I have forgotten? I need to talk to Locke now."

****

ALBATROSS UNIT

Locke stood in his office, staring at a screen as the video chat session initialized. As the video commenced, Locke saw a half-naked Eugene bouncing across the floor as he pulled up his pants. Locke noticed rather immediately that the room did not resemble any room in Eugene's loft. He quickly pointed his remote to another screen and brought up the live footage of Eugene's apartment. According to that monitor, Eugene was up late watching an old broadcast of a cartoon called Rick and Morty.

"Son of a bitch! Where the hell are you right now, and why don't I know about it?" Eugene pulled a shirt over his head and then sat down closer to the camera.

"That doesn't matter right now, Director. I've got actionable data that you need to get your people on asap!" Locke pushed a call button for his chief analyst.

"What's the source?"

"A witness that didn't make it. Listen, Secretary of State, Lisa Pennet, was receiving calls from a contact with M.O.R.S. She was recruited by someone high up in the organization, and she agreed because she went to college with this woman. I didn't get a name, but if we could cross reference the names of her graduating classes throughout her education with the names we've acquired through the recovered M.O.R.S. data, we might be able to find a match."

"I'll get my best people on it. Good work, although I'll need you to fill in some details when we next debrief." Locke saw Juliet step into frame as she buttoned up a shirt. "Ms. Cubro, it is good to see you alive after the Utah raid. A simple call would have been nice."

"My apologies, Director. It took me some time to recuperate, and then I had a matter to which I needed to attend. Good work on dropping the bomb on the facility. Unfortunately, by that point, the rest of my team was dead." Juliet looked away from the camera for a moment. "They were good agents, Director."

"I know they were, and you all performed admirably. I saw the footage, and I'm sorry it went down like that. With the video tour up and running, we had a chance to extrapolate some data through the hotspots generated by each agent's personal link. We didn't get much, but we were able to get something." Juliet nodded, glad to hear that something was recovered from the mission.

"Any thoughts on the crops, Director. I doubt they were simply raising their own food down there."

"Sadly the MOAB blew that compound to hell, and our second team wasn't able to recover any of it to sample. I've got people looking over our data for any agriculture references. I agree, though, that it's concerning." Locke looked at another screen with status update on all projects. "While you two were off grid, our analysts found Echelon's current active form. Just like I predicted earlier, it looks like

M.O.R.S. is still using this massive beast of a program to spy on any and all unsecured communications across the globe, as well as transmit their own data safely through it. I've got a team trying to crack it as we speak, if we can secure access, I believe I can find a location for their base. Tell me where you are, and I can have a transport pick you up. Hopefully by then I can have a location for you and a team to hit."

16 DO YOU WANT TO LIVE?

ALBATROSS UNIT

"I've got something, Director!" Chief Analyst Bradley Detton came running up the stairs and into Locke's office like a bat out of hell. He stopped for a second to catch his breath and then grabbed the monitor remote off of the table. "May I, sir?"

"Go ahead, Detton." Detton plugged in a flash drive to the side of the large monitor and brought up a map of North America.

"Ok, so check this out. In the heart of North Dakota, there's this outright war between four small towns. Rugby, Balta, Robinson and Center, North Dakotans all believe that they are, in fact, the geological center of North America. Rugby actually had a monument erected in its town to declare their status after a U.S. Geological Survey mathematician made the determination in 1928. Since then, however, one study after another has declared one of the other three towns to be a more accurate calculation. Lawsuits surrounding registered names and trademarks have pitted the towns against each other for decades." Detton stopped for a moment, fascinated by the history of it all.

"I appreciate a history lesson as much as the next man, Agent, but I'm going to need you to get to the point."

"Right, right, of course. I think we were able to breach one of Echelon's subprotocols. We used that to search for a prominent portal, access point, or a hotspot of some kind where the majority of data was being reported to. We cross referenced that with the less decipherable data from Panama and Utah, and it appeared to generate a specific longitude and latitude that landed right next to this four-town dispute. There's a small mountain range called White Butte, which appears to be the former center of the North American continent, before erosion shaved off some of the coasts. It would seem that M.O.R.S. is operating out of a structure at the base of that mountain range."

"Listen, we're gonna have to work on your long-winded build up speeches that hold little to no relevance to the information that you're trying to relay. Still, good work Detton. Keep working on the Echelon breach. I want as much data as we can pull from that." As Detton left the office, Locke pushed a speed dial button on his phone to reach one of his pilots. "Once you pick up Juliet and Eugene, I've got landing coordinates in North Dakota. You'll need to take the team there and stick around for air support. By the time you arrive, I should have some satellite data and hopefully county records that show some kind of structure. I want Juliet and Eugene to each have a satellite phone and an ear piece so I can reach them if needed."

****

NORTH DAKOTA

Juliet sat across from Eugene in the cargo hold of the Osprey. She looked down the bay at the rest of the twenty or so Agents, each preparing for the raid. She couldn't help but think of her last team, of Agent Yoke and his crew, and how they had each had their own pre-mission ritual; listening to an old school screamo track from Linkin Park, praying, sharpening knives, or playing cards with a fellow comrade. This new group was no different, but Juliet hoped they wouldn't meet a similar fate. It was only slightly easier, to know each of the previous team members personally, but she could hear their screams of agony when she closed her eyes. So, she kept her eyes open instead, peering into Eugene's.

"You good?" Eugene looked concerned, like he could see through her, to the worries she was trying not to focus on. Thankfully, their headsets were on a private circuit, so the rest of the team couldn't hear. She might still be just a consultant for Albatross, but she found herself more and more concerned about those around her than just her own well-being. She could have teleported out of that bunker in Utah at the first sign of trouble, but she stayed behind in an attempt to save the lives of the men and women who had joined her on the raid. Perhaps this was an admirable quality in some people's eyes, but Juliet couldn't help to also consider it a weakness. Until now, she had looked out for herself alone and for Eugene from afar. She didn't need more distractions, more connections or commitments; not if she wanted to survive.

"I'm good." Juliet looked down to see Eugene's skull helmet resting on the floor and chuckled. "You brought that thing along?"

"It's a bit more than a Halloween mask. This thing is made from the highest grade of bullet proof body armor. It's saved my life more than a few times over the last couple weeks." Eugene smiled and slapped the helmet a few times like a bongo drum. "At this point I don't think I could go into battle without it."

"As much as I'm not looking forward to a battle, I'm hoping we don't find another abandoned…" Juliet was cut off as an explosion rocked the side of the Osprey as the craft began to spin.

"This is the pilot. We've been hit! The rocket collided with our left proprotor. We're going down! Brace for impact!"

The team struggled to hold on as a couple of agents that weren't buckled in suddenly hit the ceiling of the craft and were thrown from side to side. Juliet closed her eyes, focusing on the dark to block out the vertigo inducing spinning of the craft. She knew the Osprey would hit the ground at any moment, but hated that she didn't have a window to see it. She felt the spinning begin to slow as she assumed the pilot was attempting to right the craft before the crash. The Osprey pulled up at the last minute and hit the ground with the back of its belly. The right wing broke off on impact as the aircraft skidded to a halt.

"We're alive, team, but not for much longer if we don't get the hell out of this bird!" Juliet stood up and took command of the group. "Let's go! Let's go! Get the hell up before we all die!"

Juliet checked on the pilot as her team forced the door open to the outside. The pilot and his co-pilot were dead; both holding their controls with a firm grip. As Juliet disembarked the craft, she saw that they had landed in a field just south of the mountain and the compound. Seven Ospreys and a few other helicopters flew overhead, opening fire on the compound. As their downed aircraft exploded behind them, Juliet, Eugene, and the rest of the crew began to run toward the compound beginning their assault.

****

ALBATROSS UNIT

"Director, the assault teams have arrived at the North Dakota facility. One bird is down, but minimal casualties. The main assault is underway." Detton stood in Locke's door as he delivered the update.

"Good. What have we found in reference to Eugene's tip regarding Secretary Pennet?"

"We're still running a cross-reference, but nothing to report back yet. If something pings, I have it set to appear on your desktop." Suddenly, an alarm sounded overhead as red lights turned on across the command center. Locke pulled up the security feeds for the outside of the building and saw several trucks outside of the teddy-bear warehouse full of M.O.R.S. attack teams. "That's right outside! How did they find us?"

"Probably piggybacking through Echelon, just like we found them." Locke grabbed his phone and pressed the base-wide intercom. "Attention all, this is the Director. We're about to be breached. All hands to the armory. Get your gear and get ready. We've got the enemy knocking on our door, ladies and gentleman. Let's show them a good time."

****

NORTH DAKOTA

Juliet took cover behind the crashed helicopter as the bullets zipped overhead. Most of the team had made it across the perimeter of the compound and were joined with other teams that landed after the crash. The compound at the base of the mountain was made up of several small trailer sized buildings that surrounded one large white dome that stood several stories tall and looked to be large enough to hold a department store or two inside. Juliet ducked out from cover and pulled the trigger of her assault rifle, putting two M.O.R.S. guards down. She saw Eugene advancing to the side of one of the trailers. Jumping to her feet, Juliet opened fire at a mass of guards as she ran for the trailer. Eugene provided cover fire until Juliet made it safely by his side.

"This is taking too long. We need a team to cut through these lackey guards and get to the dome." Juliet nodded in agreement as she turned and signaled for a group of Albatross agents to make their way to the trailer. Once they had gathered about ten agents, Juliet signaled for a Vee assault formation, and led the charge. Eugene joined the ten agents as they rounded the corner of the trailer and commenced firing on any opposing forces they could see.

Holding a tight formation, like a flock a geese, the team cut down all M.O.R.S. agents in their path. While more Albatross agents filed in behind them to cover the rear, Juliet's team cut a hole in M.O.R.S.'s ground level defenses and made a run for the dome. As one of the trailers exploded from an air strike behind them, Juliet's team found an entrance to the dome and all agents took defensive positions as Eugene rigged the door to blow.

"Feel free to kill anything that moves in there, but be on the lookout for one of our own. Agent Riley Harper could very well be held hostage somewhere inside." Juliet looked down at Eugene as he placed the charges, admiring his optimism. "Ready to blow! Take cover!"

Juliet joined her team on the ground as the door exploded outward. Juliet covered their six, shooting two advancing M.O.R.S. guards and one sniper lying on top of a trailer as the rest of the team breached the dome. Once inside, the team came to a halt. There was nothing inside; not one building, one guard, no pile of supplies or weapons.

"What...What the hell is this?" Eugene scanned the area, looking for something on the walls near the door. "Juliet, can you sense anything?"

"There's something here, I just can't see it." Juliet walked forward as her internal network scanned for something to hack into. Suddenly, Juliet's earpiece rang as her Sat Phone was receiving a call.

"This is Juliet, go." Juliet heard gunfire and explosions in the background.

"Juliet, it's Locke. We're under attack at the home base. M.O.R.S. tracked our signal back and sent quite a hefty force to take us out." She heard Locke groan in pain and then yell something angrily in Korean as he fired a machine gun. "I don't think we're going to make it here, but I needed to get word to you. We came up with a name based on Eugene's info of Secretary Pennet's past. I doubled check it, and unlikely as it sounds, it's the only possibility. The name of the person seemingly behind all this is…."

****

Eugene watched as Juliet kept walking straight ahead from the breached door, toward the center of the dome, until she suddenly disappeared about thirty feet away.

"Juliet!" Eugene and his men advanced forward after Juliet. When they reached the spot where she had last stood, they suddenly crossed through an invisible barrier into an area of the dome completely hidden from where they were standing earlier. "Holy shit, they have camouflage technology."

Now, instead of a completely empty dome, the rest of the oval shaped surface was filled with power conductors, computers, general operation tents, transport trucks, and a ton of M.O.R.S. soldiers all pointing there rifles in Eugene's direction. Eugene saw Juliet with her hands up, and followed suit. She had a distressed look on her face, but it didn't seem to be due to the M.O.R.S. soldiers. As the rest of the agents were put on their knees and stripped of their weapons, Eugene found himself looking up and around, awestruck at the setup. He figured the camouflage barrier must not hold up to well vertically, otherwise they wouldn't need the dome to shield this area from satellite view.

Eugene and Juliet were brought to their feet, handcuffed, and escorted further into the center of the dome. Eugene could see two tunnel entrances on the other side going off into the side of the mountain. While M.O.R.S. continued to impress Eugene with their ability to set up shop underground, he quickly found something else to focus on. In the middle of the dome stood two tall black pillars, each about twenty feet high, standing ten feet or so apart. All of the electronic equipment in the dome seemed to be centered around these two pillars, but nothing seemed to be necessarily connected to them. As they got closer, Eugene saw a woman on her knees near the base of the pillars, chained to a metal pole.

"Riley!" The woman raised her head at Eugene's call, revealing her face and most of her body to be badly bruised and discolored. Riley looked at Eugene with confusion on her face, and only then did Eugene remember that he was still wearing his skull mask. Unable to take it off with his hands cuffed behind him, Eugene turned to Juliet for help, Juliet however was looking at someone else, a woman standing at an upright console on the opposite side of the pillars. As Eugene was placed on his knees next to Riley, the woman turned and faced him, leaving him speechless.

"Finally! The time has finally come when I have the pleasure of meeting the acclaimed and accomplished assassin known as Juliet Cubro. And yes, to sweeten the occasion, Mr. Bones has arrived as well! Both of you have proven quite the adversaries for the House of M.O.R.S. It's an honor to meet you both!"

"Wait, this can't be happening."

"Oh I assure you that it is happening, Mr. Bones." The woman stepped forward accompanied by a man in a back uniform, looked at Eugene and cocked her head to the side. "My apologies, Mr. Bones, but I simply can't wait any longer. My general here and I must know the face of the deviant who's killed so many of our colleges."

"No," but the woman ignored Eugene's plea and pulled off the helmet. Her look of immense satisfaction quickly turned to shock as she stepped back.

"Eugene?" The woman stepped back, stunned to see Eugene's cross face staring back at her. She looked down at him for a moment, and then quickly grabbed her handgun and pointed it at her general. "You would put my son's life in danger?"

"I didn't know, I swear it," but the general's

pleading went on deaf ears as the woman pulled the trigger and shot the man in the face. She looked back at Eugene, crouching down before him and staring into his eyes.

"Eugene. How can this be?"

"HOW ARE YOU ALIVE?! WHO ARE YOU?!" Eugene gritted his teeth as he yelled into the woman's face, demanding an answer.

"I'm your mother, Eugene. Don't you recognize me?" Riley looked up, squinting through her swollen left eye.

"You're Jane Reynolds?"

"No, she's not. My mother died in a car wreck when I was a child. I saw the body, I watched her take her final breath." Eugene forced himself up from the ground, hands still cuffed behind him, and screamed at the woman. "NOW, WHO ARE YOU?"

"I'm sorry, baby, but you're wrong. You didn't see me die that night. You saw a replica of me, made at a plant similar to the one that made your friend Juliet over here." One of the M.O.R.S. guards kicked the back of Eugene's legs and sent him back down into the dirt, as the woman leaned in and brushed his cheek with her hand. "But I'm the real thing, honey, and I've never stopped loving you, or looking out for you. I swear it."

"Even if I believed you, that doesn't explain why you're so surprised to see me here with Albatross."

"Oh I knew you were playing hero with Albatross, I just didn't know you were Mr. Bones. In fact, when I didn't see you among the invasion teams, all of which have now been detained or killed, I figured you were hanging out back at the teddy bear factory with Director Locke and all his pals. Oh yes, we found your little hideout. My men are currently there now, looking for you and killing the rest."

"You're a liar! I don't believe you! You haven't done shit for me since I grew up." Eugene spit on the ground at her feet. Juliet watched as she proceeded to break her thumb enough to slide out of her handcuffs. "This is all just a ruse; some sort of sick game."

"It's not a game sweetheart. Who do you think fixed the murder hearings to get you acquitted of all charges? Who maintained the steady flow of cash and stocks into your account from Reynolds Pharmaceuticals? Why do you think those men showed up at Summerhill right after this little redheaded tramp showed up and disturbed you?"

"Those men tried to kill me!"

"They weren't there to kill you! They were there to kill anyone who had seen you, yes, but they were also there to rescue you! I had planned to bring you into the fold back then, but these two worthless bitches got in the way!" The woman crouched down again in front of Eugene, her knees now in the dirt next to his. "I know this is all a shock, and I didn't plan on breaking it to you like this, but it's true! Sweetheart, I'm your mother! You're my son! And no matter the circumstances, I couldn't be more happy to see you here, at this monumental moment!"

"Riley. Are you alright?" Riley was wearing tattered nurse scrubs, stained in blood and other things. She raised her head a bit to smile through the pain at Eugene.

"Oh little Ms. Harper over here just couldn't be a model prisoner. Even after I offered her some finer comforts, and some quality solid food, she still tried to escape. She actually killed three of my men with a plastic fork!" Jane Reynolds kicked Riley in the chest, causing her to fall onto her back. "So I allowed my men to beat her to a pulp, but only to a pulp, as I wanted her alive and conscious for this day."

"You sadistic bitch!" Juliet, with her hands free, grabbed a blade from either boot and shoved them into the knees of the guards standing behind her. As they fell to the ground, Juliet retrieved the knives and threw them into two more guards advancing on her. She turned around and lunged at Jane, but was tackled from a blind spot on her left. The guard held her down long enough for another guard to stick the back of her neck with a stun stick. Her body convulsed a bit with the high voltage. She tried to get to her feet, reaching for Jane, but was struck with a higher dosage of electricity, and soon collapsed to the ground.

"And stay down," Jane said as she kicked Juliet square in the gut.

"Don't touch her! Don't you touch her." Eugene struggled to defend his love, but was held down by the guard behind him. Jane looked back at Eugene, a sarcastic frown on her face.

"Oh how sweet is this? My little boy has fallen in love with the assassin that killed his dad. You're more messed up than I thought you were, kid!" Jane stepped away from Juliet as two guards picked up her limp body and dragged her away. "Oh don't worry, baby. I won't be the one touching her. No sir, that job belongs to my faithful and loyal friend, Dr. Hanes. He's longed so much to reunite with his lost toy."

"No!" Eugene managed to get to his feet but was immediately punched in the gut and sent back down to the ground. He struggled to catch his breath as tears began to flow. "I… I don't understand. I don't understand any of this."

"Oh, sweetheart I know you don't. Of course you don't!" Jane stood next to her boy, running her hands through his sweaty hair. "In due time, darling, I promise you'll understand.

"But first, we have some business to take care of. I'd like to introduce you to another of my personal colleges, Dr. Lawrence Obasi. A child of Nigeria, Obasi left his homeland to go to school at Oxford. First he studied Agriculture, hoping to learn how to expand the worth of his native country's soil. Then, he got a taste for business and decided he did not want to return to his broken home. Instead, he founded the second largest commercial agricultural firm in the world." Obasi stepped forward and shook Jane's hand.

"While my company's four principal business segments are Seed & Grain, Crop Protection, Nutrients & Merchandise, and Rural Services, we also have ties to dairy farming and livestock." Obasi smiled and stepped over to a table with several monitors.

"He operates out of China, and does extremely well for himself. His company's reach is incredibly vast, and thus he was the perfect business partner for the House of M.O.R.S. You see the crops that your friend Juliet stumbled on in Utah were a test grow of Obasi's newest nutrient-filled seed stock. Obasi worked with Stoke to bioengineer his seeds to include a strain of our experimental formula; a very high concentration of the black goo that Stoke was injecting into his test subjects. The same black goo that Agent Harper here came across in Seattle.

"So they put that stuff in the seeds of all of these crops, but masked it so that the average human body wouldn't react to it without being triggered by something else. Then we worked on the triggers." Jane seemed so eager to tell Eugene about how they planned to end the world, that she barely took a moment to breathe. "For years now, agricultural companies have been injecting genetically altered Bacillus Thuringiensis, into crops to keep the pests away. The Bt genes switch on in pollen, green tissue, and other parts of the crop seed and develop over time as the seeds grow. So Obasi and Stoke modified those synthetic Bt genes to include triggers for our substance. Over a third of the world's population is allergic to pollen, and the rest still inhale it anyway. But for those that don't eat crops with insecticides, Obasi also distributed the genes to his friends across the world in the clean water business. Now, tap water around the world is constantly being treated with a large numbers of chemicals, to include liquefied Chlorine, Fluorosilicic Acid, and Calcium Hydroxide, in order to kill bacteria and microorganisms. Obasi and Stoke added their own concoction to the mix.

"Look at me. I'm boring the hell out of my son and his co-worker as I ramble on about all this science crap. The point of all this, children, is that starting today, these infected crops and other plants will begin to be harvested and distributed around the world. The new water treatments will begin today as well. The engineered pollen will take flight, so that the average human will either inhale or ingest one or several of our chemical cocktails. Now it won't be as immediate as the girls that died in Seattle, but by the end of next week, two weeks at the latest, two thirds of the population will be infected and will begin to show signs of deterioration. A small portion of the populace will be naturally immune to our attacks, and the rest will be provided a life preserver of sorts." Another man stepped into view and hugged Jane. "And that's where this man, Hernando Rivera, the current head of Reynolds Pharmaceuticals, steps in. Hernando took the reins of my company after my supposed death.

"Under my authority, Reynolds Pharmaceuticals has been developing both a vaccine for those we deem worthy of surviving and flourishing after the cleansing, and a temporary inhalant for those we deem worthy of serving after the cleaning. The vaccine has already been administered to the right people across the planet, and the inhalant will release on the market in the coming weeks. It is designed to suppress the toxins that, by then, will be flourishing in a majority of the human populace. Should someone forego regular dosages of said inhalant, they would then succumb to their illness. This way we will keep the underclass in check when it's time to move on and rebuild."

"Why…" Riley grunted and immediately winced in pain, as she came back to a kneeling position beside Eugene.

"Oh I'm sorry, darling, you're going to have to speak up a bit.

"Why? Why are you doing this? Clearly there's more to it than what was disclosed in Stoke's raving manifesto. Why do you wish to take out such a huge percentage of the population?"

"The why is not really any of your concern." Riley leaned over onto Eugene's arm for support. Eugene leaned his head against hers and then sat up to continue Riley's line of questioning.

"Then how did you come across this technology? Juliet told me that Stoke and Hanes were taught how to accomplish these things, how to design these technological and bioengineered wonders. I refuse to believe that you, and only you with the House of M.O.R.S. suddenly came up with all these achievements in science and anatomy." Jane whispered something into Obasi's ear and then turned back to Eugene.

"You always were the clever one, my little Eugene. You're right to question these things, and that's why I brought you here to meet the final member of our organization. The "M" of M.O.R.S., Dr. Michelle Reynolds." Dr. Obasi entered a few key strokes into the his console and suddenly the two pillars became alive, as screeching bolts of electricity shot back and forth between thm. The intensity of the electricity grew as the bolts grew thicker and longer, expanding from several small bolts into a few large overlapping ones. Finally, a complete wall of bluish white light filled the ten foot space between the tall pillars. A figure emerged from the wall of light; a woman with a striking resemblance to Jane. "When I was born, I was supposed to be a twin, and my parents were going to name my sister Michelle. Unfortunately, Michelle died during birth. This

Michelle, however, is from a place where she survived, but her twin baby sister Jane did not."

"Wait." Riley had a confused and annoyed look on her face. "Are you saying she's from an alternate universe or something?"

"Quick study, Agent Riley! Top marks to you!" Jane and Michelle exchanged hugs. "Thank you for joining us, Michelle! This is the first day of the cleansing, and we couldn't have come this far without you."

"Ugh my head hurts," moaned Riley as she leaned back against the legs of the guard standing behind her. Suddenly, she reached up and grabbed the guard's hands, twisting her body and leaning back, Riley propelled her legs up into the air to wrap around the neck of the guard. As she brought him down to the ground, she unlocked the cuffs with the keys from his belt. By the time he hit the ground, Riley was standing with his Beretta AR70 assault rifle in her hands. She dropped the keys next to Eugene and then aimed her rifle at the two women. "Perhaps it's the pain that I'm already dealing with, but I'm having a hard time believing this tall tale your spinning. So I suggest you tell your man Obasi to reverse whatever things you've put in play, and we all ease off of this whole cleansing bullshit."

"Oh I'm sorry, you delusional bunny, but there's nothing we can do to stop what's already in motion." Jane and Michelle stood there in confidence while the group was swarmed by more armed M.O.R.S. guards.

"I don't believe it, but since you're unwilling to cooperate, I might as well just off the both of you and give us all of a break from your never ending monotonous speeches." But before Riley could pull the trigger, Eugene's hand slid over the top of the rifle and slowly pushed it down. "What? What the hell are you doing?"

"I'm sorry, Riley. Clearly there are larger forces at play here. We have to admit that we've lost." Eugene took the rifle from Riley's weak hands, and backed away from her as he released the magazine and ejected the bullet from the chamber. Tossing the rifle to the ground he clasped his hands together and pleaded with Riley. "I know this isn't ideal, and it's not what we wanted, but at the end of the day it comes down to one thing. Do you want to live?"

"Is this a joke? These people just killed all of our peers back at Albatross! You're going to let them get away with that?"

"What peers, Riley? Look at yourself. You've been missing for almost a month now! Locke didn't seem like he was in a rush to find you. The majority of the crew, in fact, was working off the assumption that you were dead! I had to wear that stupid mask to get any work done, because Locke was too chickenshit to make any real moves to find you!" Riley collapsed to the ground as she shook her head.

"Is this who you really are, Eugene? A selfish prick concerned only about his own existence?"

"I'm a realist, Riley. I always have been. Now I was more than willing to play along with you and Locke's band of misfits, but playtime is over. We lost, Riley! Locke lost! You lost!" Jane smiled at her son, nodding her head in agreement.

"Finally someone is talking sense around here. Well said, son, well said." Eugene fell down on his knees next to Riley and grabbed her hand in his.

"I don't know who she is. If she truly is my mother, she's been missing the majority of my life. But let's face the facts here. We could die like the rest of the world, or we could find a way to live after all the dust settles." He put his head closer to Riley's, pleading with her. "If there's a way for me to save you, I will. I want you. Let me try to save you. You can hate me, you can avoid me when it's all said and done, but if I join them I might be able to keep you breathing. I mean that's what it really boils down to, right? Do you or do you not want to live?"

"Ask and you shall receive, Eugene. I don't personally care for her, but if you wish it, we can spare her life. We'll lock her up and keep her healthy, and then add her to the working class when we begin to rebuild this society." Jane smiled at the thought, and giggled a bit next to Michelle.

"Yes, Eugene, and I would love to get to know you more, myself. I, unfortunately lost my Eugene years ago to an irreversible illness. To spend time with you would be a honor and a pleasure beyond bounds for me." Michelle took Jane's hand in hers and squeezed it tight. "Clearly you have unresolved issues with your mother, but that's nothing that time cannot fix. While we rid this world of all its uselessness, you can grow to know your mother again."

Eugene looked at the two ladies, at the pillars of light, and then at the rest of the dome; taking in the magnitude of M.O.R.S. and knowing that there was still so much he did not understand. Riley was right. Ever since his father died, he reduced his needs for morality and compassion. He looked out for himself back then, and now he needed to lookout for himself now. If Juliet were here, even if she didn't want to admit it, he knew her heart was just as cold as his. Perhaps he could arrange a deal for her, and if not, at least she would be alive somewhere. Eugene looked down at Riley's exhausted face, watching as she used every bit of her strength to grip his hand and beg him not to give in.

"Please Eugene, don't do this. If we die, we die. But at least we wouldn't have to succumb to their treachery. Please, Eugene." Eugene shook his head and pried Riley's fingers from his hand.

"I'm sorry, Riley, but I'm not ready to die today." Riley's expression turned to shock, and then to anger as she dug her fingernails into his skin.

"No! You son of a bitch! How dare you! After all they've done! After all we did for you! After all I did for you! Damn you, Eugene! DAMN YOU!" Eugene flicked her hands again and stood up to face his mother.

"Will you spare our lives if I join you?" Jane smiled at his request and opened her arms as she stepped forward.

"Oh darling. I would never hurt a hair on your head." She wrapped her arms around him and hugged him tightly as Eugene slowly lifted his arms and hugged her in return. Tucking his head into her shoulder, he recognized her smell, the same sweet smell he had remembered from when he was a kid.

This was truly his mother, and amidst his frustration, he couldn't deny the joy he was experiencing in that moment.

"Now go with these men into the mountain, and wait for me, child. There's so much I have to tell you." Jane took Eugene under her wing and guided him over to a couple of guards. She raised a finger toward them and stared at each of them. "You will respect my son, and treat him like the family he is.

"Obasi, my friend, Michelle here is going to be staying with us for a while to oversee the following weeks of progression. Let's close up the portal for now." Jane looked over at Riley, shriveled up in defeat on the ground. "You three guards dispense of this filth. I want her dead and discarded somewhere where I won't see her ugly mug again."

"No! No, mother! You promised!" Eugene struggled against the guards who held him back and pulled him towards a jeep to ascend the mountain tunnel. "You promised me!"

"I'm sorry, darling, but some promises aren't meant to be kept." Jane escorted Michelle away from the pillars and toward the exit of the dome, as the guards forced Eugene into the back seat of the jeep and drove away towards the tunnel.

****

Riley heard Eugene's pathetic screams as she struggled to her feet. The space around her was blurry and discolored as she tried to balance herself. She saw Dr. Obasi make his way back to the terminal to close the border and reached out to stop him, but he was at least twenty feet away from her and her perception was all out of whack. As the guards began to pick her up and drag her away from the pillars, Riley saw a man in a white coat loading Juliet's unconscious body into the back of a truck and heading for the second tunnel into the mountain.

Riley began to realize that this was her end. Her friend had betrayed her, her ally was begin carted off somewhere to be reprogramed and abused, her superior was likely dead in the Albatross bunker, and the rest of the world was currently on the road to obliteration. Still, she would have struggled free and went out guns blazing if she had the strength to do so, but she didn't. Riley fell back into the arms of her executioners as they dragged her away from the bright light between the pillars.

Before Riley lost the strength to keep her eyes open, however, she noticed sparks of color erupting from the wall of light between the pillar. Beams of light were shooting outward from the portal and hitting whatever they came in contact with on the other side. Riley fought to stay awake as she noticed Dr. Obasi begin to panic and call for guards to assist him. As several armed men took position in front of the pillars, more stray beams of light sprung out from the portal; some hitting the guards, causing them to fall over in death.

Suddenly, three people emerged from the portal, all firing energy based weapons as they shot their way through the file of soldiers. Two of the shooters went after Dr. Obasi, as the third fired upon the guards holding Riley. As they fell to the ground around her, they slowly came into view. A woman knelt down in front of Riley and grabbed her hand. Riley struggled against her blurry vision to see the face of her liberator. The woman had red hair, a face full of freckles, and an eye patch over her right eye; it was as if Riley was staring into a mirror.

"Riley, it's me. I'm Riley, I'm you from another place. I don't know if you understand me, but I need you to trust me." The woman helped Riley to her feet and carried her to a jeep while the other two hopped in the back and laid down cover fire. "Where's Obasi?"

"He got away. We don't have time, we have to get out of here!" The woman sighed in disappointment and then stepped on the gas. One of the men in the back of the jeep threw a grenade at the terminal by the still active pillars. As the explosion destroyed the terminal and the pillars behind them, the woman stepped on the gas and rammed the loading door.

The men in back continued to fire on any and all targets until the jeep had cleared the compound and began making its way across the North Dakota plains. Riley struggled to speak A she sat strapped down to the passenger seat, staring at the mirror image of herself driving the car. The woman turned and grabbed hold of Riley's arm, squeezing it softly.

"What the hell is going on?" Riley could barely croak out her words.

"Don't worry, Riley. We've got you. These men and I are part of the resistance. We have to get you somewhere safe, and then I'll tell you everything."

"Watch the road, Riles. We're not in the clear yet." The woman looked in the rearview mirror back at the compound as several M.O.R.S. vehicles were beginning their pursuit. She turned again to Riley, a look of concern on her face. She grabbed Riley by the arm again, trying to assure her through touch, what her words were trying to convey.

"I know you're confused, and I know you're in pain, but you're gonna get through this. I swear we'll make this all right somehow." The woman scanned her rear view again, then looked back down at Riley. "This isn't over, Riley. Trust me."

Riley Harper and company will return soon
in final chapter of the Fierce Saga:
The Fury of the Fierce.

The Fierce Will Fall

ABOUT THE AUTHOR

Joshua D. Howell, out of Omaha, Nebraska, wrote his first novel in high school and published it while serving overseas in the military. After traveling the world, he returned to civilian life and ultimately to his writing roots. Since publishing the first book in the Fierce Saga, Joshua has traveled the country to several comic conventions and book expos to meet his fans and make new ones. He has received awards for several works of poetry, as well as for a few short stories published in various fiction anthologies. He has a deep passion for all things media; film, literature, and music. He especially adores the mysteries of science fiction. This novel marks the third book published under the Fierce Literature imprint; the first being the graphic novel adaption of The Fierce Are Fading.

Joshua D. Howell